Praise for <u>The Last True Love Story</u>

★"Readers will be swept up in Kiely's musical prose as Teddy learns about love, romance, forgiveness, and reconciliation."
—*Kirkus Reviews*, starred review

★"Poetic, lovely, and profound . . . Satisfying and full of longing, the book features deep feelings, full hearts, and heartbreak. It speaks to the importance of forging connections and the power of story to capture memories and meaning."
—*VOYA*, starred review

★"A sophisticated story about the power of love, music, and making amends. Deeply personal and universal at the same time, Kiely's truly lovely tale should find a home in every YA collection."
—*School Library Journal*, starred review

"Genuine, thoughtful, and heartbreaking, *The Last True Love Story* is the kind of book that kick-starts an awakening in your soul and will resonate with readers for years to come."
—Julie Murphy, *New York Times* bestselling author of *Dumplin'* and *Side Effects May Vary*

"Brendan Kiely's writing soars off the page, ultimately landing someplace between heartwarming and heart-aching (but definitely somewhere in the heart). Here is a book about music, friendship, first and final loves, and all the blue notes in between. Indeed, *The Last True Love Story* may be exactly that."
—David Arnold, bestselling author of *Kids of Appetite* and *Mosquitoland*

"As cool as it is tender, this poignant story about the power of love thrums with classic rock and aches with honesty. I was so moved by Hendrix's journey and, as a brown girl who loves music, I was completely invested in Corrina—one of my new favorite characters in all of YA. Authentic and beautifully written, *The Last True Love Story* will truly capture your heart."
—Jasmine Warga, author of *My Heart and Other Black Holes*

"A beautiful, searing journey into the American heartland. This book, like an epic road trip, is full of difficult truths, great music, and deeply human companions."
—Daniel José Older, award-winning author of *Shadowshaper* and the Bone Street Rumba series

"Some authors write with their hearts first and their heads second. Some the other way around. But Brendan Kiely manages, as always, to strike a skillful and delicate balance between deep, intellectual coming-of-age and poetic, emotional drama. *The Last True Love Story* stands in a league of its own both in regards to the way it portrays its teenage protagonists and the way it tells the very personal, tragic story of Alzheimer's. If the point of living is learning how to love, to quote Gpa, then I think we should all start by reading Mr. Kiely's beautiful novel."

—John Corey Whaley, winner of the Printz and Morris awards, National Book Award finalist, and author of *Highly Illogical Behavior*

"*The Last True Love Story* is a tender multigenerational story that's as much about the meaning of family as it is about falling in love. There's plenty of delightful adventure, but what I loved most about this book is its respect for moments that can be both quiet and life changing at once."

—Ava Dellaira, author of *Love Letters to the Dead*

"A quirky, romantic, and satisfying story."   —*Publishers Weekly*

"This bittersweet, sometimes humorous coming-of-age journey hits all the right notes, with its emotional language, vivid landscapes, and quirky characters. . . . A good fit for new adults, graduates of Joan Bauer's *Rules of the Road*, or those who enjoyed John Green's *Looking for Alaska*." —*Booklist*

"The story seamlessly integrates family history and the present, creating a tale of love free from cheesiness. Raw, imperfect relationships will strike a chord with teenage readers. Part road trip, part romance, this story is the stuff of summer dreams. Recommended."   —*School Library Connection*

Also by Brendan Kiely

The Gospel of Winter

All American Boys
(coauthored with Jason Reynolds)

BRENDAN KIELY

THE LAST TRUE LOVE STORY

MARGARET K. McELDERRY BOOKS
NEW YORK   LONDON   TORONTO   SYDNEY   NEW DELHI

For Grandma and for Jessie,
who teach me how to live with a listening heart

>ᵔ⌒ᵔ<

MARGARET K. McELDERRY BOOKS
An imprint of Simon & Schuster Children's Publishing Division
1230 Avenue of the Americas, New York, New York 10020

MARGARET K. McELDERRY BOOKS is a trademark of Simon & Schuster, Inc.
For information about special discounts for bulk purchases, please contact Simon & Schuster Special Sales at 1-866-506-1949 or business@simonandschuster.com.
The Simon & Schuster Speakers Bureau can bring authors to your live event. For more information or to book an event, contact the Simon & Schuster Speakers Bureau at 1-866-248-3049 or visit our website at www.simonspeakers.com.
Also available in a Margaret K. McElderry Books hardcover edition
The text for this book was set in Calluna.
Manufactured in the United States of America
First Margaret K. McElderry Books paperback edition September 2017
2 4 6 8 10 9 7 5 3 1
The Library of Congress has cataloged the hardcover edition as follows:
Names: Kiely, Brendan, 1977– author.
Title: Last true love story / Brendan Kiely.
Description: First edition. | New York : Margaret K. McElderry Books, [2016].
Summary: "Hendrix and Corrina bust Hendrix's grandfather out of assisted. living, and leave LA for New York in pursuit of freedom, truth, and love" —Provided by publisher.
Identifiers: LCCN 2015036953
ISBN 978-1-4814-2988-7 (hc)
ISBN 978-1-4814-2989-4 (pbk)
ISBN 978-1-4814-2990-0 (eBook)
Subjects: | CYAC: Love—Fiction. | Self-realization—Fiction. | Grandfathers—Fiction. | Alzheimer's disease—Fiction.
Classification: LCC PZ7.K5398 Las 2016 | DDC [Fic]—dc23
LC record available at lccn.loc.gov/2015036953

That Love is all there is,
Is all we know of Love.

—EMILY DICKINSON,
FROM "THE SINGLE HOUND"

Wise as you will have become, so full of experience,
you will have understood by then what these Ithakas mean.

—C. P. CAVAFY,
FROM "ITHAKA"

"Every love story

LAS VEGAS

GALLUP

CADILLAC
RANCH TX

LA

FLAGSTAFF AZ

YELLOW
MOUNTAIN

BARSTOW
CA

LAGUNA
RESERVATION

is an Odyssey..."

ITHACA NY
NEW YORK

TROY IL

ST. LOUIS

TULSA OK

PROLOGUE

Here's the situation: We're lost in the desert somewhere west of Albuquerque, and the car we've stolen is nose-first in the dirt with a flat tire. Gpa, Corrina, and me. Each day that passes, my grandfather's grip on reality slips further and further away, and if I don't keep a close eye on him he might wander into the dust and disappear forever. Corrina's walked off in the other direction, so pissed she's not even talking to me, and I'm not sure she wants to go all the way across the country anymore. But I made her a promise I'd get her there. I made Gpa the same promise—to get him to see that church one last time before his disease wipes it out of his mind and all his memories of Gma are gone. All I want to do is keep these impossible promises I've made, but Mom, Corrina's parents, Gpa's doctor, the police, and the rest of the freaking known world are all out there looking for us now, and we still have over two thousand miles to go and only three days left to do it.

I'd feel like this is all coming to the end, except I can't. Because it can't be. It can't be the end, not for Gpa, not for Corrina, and not for me, because it is out here on the road in the middle of nowhere that I have finally come to understand what my grandfather means when he says the point of living is learning how to love.

PART I

How We Got There

CHAPTER 1

The Impossible Promise

The day before we busted out of town and raced into the wide, windblown roads of America, I stood three floors below Gpa's apartment, staring across the beach to the water, clutching a newly framed photo of two dead people.

Calypso Sunrise Suites Assisted Living Facility was plopped halfway between the Santa Monica Pier and the Venice Beach boardwalk, but in this strange nonlocation between the two, if nobody cruised by in front of me, and I looked past the few palm trees twisting up out of the sand, and the stretch of beach beyond them, and into the endless expanse of the Pacific—it could seem as if I was marooned on the edge of an island, lost and forgotten at sea.

At least that's how I felt as I stood there and gathered my strength to bring the photo back up to him. The week before, Gpa had smashed the glass and frame while having one of his fits, and although I'd been able to salvage the photo without it bending or tearing, I'd sliced up my palm and fingers

5

on the glass. But at least I'd saved the photo. In it, Gma, her hair whipped up in one of those sixties beehives, stood in front of their old wood-paneled station wagon, holding the bundled infant version of my dad. Gpa hadn't meant to ruin it, because it was his favorite one of her, but he'd swept it off his desk with everything else in a burst of rage, and it had shattered against the base of his floor lamp. I'd spent half an hour carefully vacuuming the area around his desk.

My hand still hurt, especially with Old Humper's leash double-wrapped around it. He was going at it with the leg of a bench along the boardwalk, but I didn't mind because I liked to let him get it out of his system before walking into Calypso, where pets were welcome, but not if they were going to get their freak on with any of the residents, guests, or staff. Still, he was small for an Amstaff, and with his dopey tongue hanging out over his teeth, the little guy could charm a smile out of a corpse. He finally grew tired and yawned to let me know, so I took him around the corner to the parking lot and up the steps to the front entrance.

None of the residents at Calypso were made of big money, but the place was still a wide, block-long, three-story complex with common rooms, an in-house bistro, an art studio, communal terraces, and a large garden off to one side, with a fountain and a few trees surrounding it, where I often met Gpa and listened to his stories, or read him poetry.

I knew most of the friendly, blue-polo-shirted staff, and I waved hello to the folks at the front desk as Old Humper and

6

I crossed the lobby. I checked the garden first—Gpa wasn't there—and then doubled back to the elevator to head up to Gpa's apartment. I knocked on the door. There was no answer, so I opened it and poked my head in.

"Damn," I said. Gpa was having another bad day.

The room was wrecked. His bed was askew, the sheets rumpled like frozen waves at the foot, and his clothes were scattered haphazardly across the floor. He had pulled and emptied the dresser drawers from the unit and tossed them toward the door to the bathroom. Even that room was destroyed. He'd flung open the cabinet doors beneath the sink and knocked his prescription bottles, shampoo, toothpaste, and deodorant into the tub.

It wasn't the real Gpa who'd done all this. It was the man who took over when he was having a fit—the man with a storm behind his eyes. A man I didn't recognize. And sometimes, when it was really bad, when he looked out at me from under his angry brow, I was afraid he might not recognize me, either. But to say it wasn't him, to say it really was someone else standing by the window in his room, was shitty on my part. It wasn't fair to say that. This *was* Gpa. I had to get used to that, and I needed to figure out how to help him.

He stood in his usual outfit, the gray slacks, the two-tone guayabera, and he had his shoes on, which was a good sign, because it meant he'd probably left the room earlier that day. He stared out the window, over the boardwalk and the sand, and gazed into the Pacific.

"Gpa," I said to his back. "Gpa, it's me, Teddy."

I let go of Old Humper's leash, and he raced over to Gpa, nuzzled his leg, then came back to me, as if looking for direction, and I wished I could give him one.

I walked across the room and repeated who I was as I approached Gpa. He kept his back to me, and I didn't want him flailing out at me suddenly, as he might, so I didn't touch him. I stepped to the side and leaned against the wall. In the late-afternoon sunlight, his cheeks were a golden sheen of tears. "Gpa," I said again.

Someone knocked on the door behind us. It opened before I could say anything, and two of Calypso's polo-shirted brigade stood in the doorway, two massive beefcakes, Julio and Frank, who looked like the football players at school who puffed out their chests when they walked and hung their arms about a foot away from their bodies like they needed to constantly air out their pits. Julio and Frank showed whenever there was Red Alert Trouble in one of the residents' rooms, or if someone was lost in the middle of the bistro, or the lobby, during one of the organized activities, or during a meal.

"Everything okay?" Julio asked, coming into the room, knowing full well it wasn't. "We need Dr. Hannaway?"

"No," I said.

Gpa breathed in and out softly and wiped at the tears on his cheeks, so I knew he'd already calmed down and the rage had passed. He was quiet because he was scared. His

8

eyes darted from me to the window and back. He probably didn't know why he'd torn up the room. It was possible he didn't even remember that he was the one who'd done it. Old Humper rubbed Gpa's shin, and Gpa bent down to scratch him.

"I got this," I told the giants.

"Doubt it," Frank said. His bald head glistened as he dipped beneath the doorframe and stepped into the room. "Charlie?" he said to Gpa.

I stepped in front of them. "Seriously." I put my hand up. "I got this. I do."

Julio frowned. He nodded to the desk with all the drawers open and the pens, paper, and magazines pushed to the carpet around it. "Come on, Teddy," he said. "We're professionals."

"And I'm family," I said back. In fact, Gpa was about all I had for family. There was Mom, of course, but she was usually gone on one business trip or another, always working, gone that week, in fact, to Shanghai, and I saw Gpa more than I saw her, even though he no longer lived with us. Mom had probably only seen him twice in the seven months since she'd stuck him at Calypso.

So it was just Gpa and me and Old Humper, because Dad was gone too, and gone for so long we never even spoke about him. My dad: dead.

"I know, buddy," Julio said. "But sometimes you have to let us handle these things. You can't do it all alone."

ulio's *buddy*. I wasn't frigging twelve, either, even
noke to me like I was on a middle school field
eventeen-year-old who was basically trying to
. ...s ramily together, or what was left of it, while the rest
of the world didn't give a flying fart if the Hendrix family
just disappeared like one of Gpa's memories: poof, as if we
never existed at all.

"Gpa," I said again. I stepped to the side, so I wouldn't
surprise or startle him. "Gpa, it's me. Teddy. We've got a job
to do."

Teddy. We've got a job to do. He must have said that a
million times to me as I was growing up. Mom was always
working. It was just me and Gpa. *Teddy. We've got a job to
do.* We would wash the kitchen floor. *Teddy. We've got a job
to do.* We would sit down and finish my essay for home-
work. *Teddy. We've got a job to do.* And we would head over
to St. Christopher's Kitchen, where we'd cook for the home-
less who washed up like driftwood on the beach and the
boardwalk.

Gpa turned from the window, and I knew he was Gpa
again. The old war hero, the disciplinarian—the half-smile
that rose in the corner of his mouth was anybody else's full
smile. The clouds had passed from his eyes.

"What are we looking for?" I asked him, risking the peace
of the moment. Julio and Frank hovered skeptically, as if they
were waiting for Gpa to take a swing so they could shout *See!
I told you so!*

"That photo," Gpa said. "The one with your grandmother standing next to our station wagon."

"Of course," I said, trying to stay as calm as possible. "Our favorite one."

Gpa nodded to me, the half-smile remaining. "Yes, exactly. *Our* favorite."

"Guys?" I said to Julio and Frank. "A little space?"

They were reluctant at first, but Gpa assured them he was fine, and I did too, and as I started to clean up the clothes, Gpa began to fix the bed. Old Humper marched a line back and forth, keeping the giants on one side and us on the other. Eventually they left, and I thought about how the tables had turned and I was helping Gpa, like a parent helps a child, just as he had helped me when he came out to fill the hole left behind by Dead Dad.

But I also still felt like a damn kid, because I didn't know what to do. As I got the dresser unit back together and put the clothes away, I couldn't decide if I should tell Gpa I had the photo or not. I could easily pretend I'd found it under the bed, or I could tell him he'd broken it last week, and I'd promised to fix it, and I had, but not fast enough—in other words, the truth, but "truth" is a fuckedupedly deceptive word when your grandfather's dying of Alzheimer's.

Gpa finished tidying the bed, pulling the sheets tight and flat and tucking the corners beneath the mattress neatly as only a marine knew how, and then stepped back to the window. "I can still see her back then," he said, looking out.

"The little silver bracelets, the flower-patterned shirt, the color of her hair. I can hear her too. Her laugh. The way she said my name." He balled his fist and shook it like he was cursing the Pacific, way out beyond the beach. "Goddamn this disease. It's going to take her away from me all over again."

I grabbed the bag by the door and joined him at the window. Even though I stood taller than Gpa, I felt so small and stupid, holding that bag with the photo of Gma, as if a photo could ever replace the real person. I put my arm around Gpa and followed his gaze out to the water and wondered if love was the thing that made us attempt the impossible, like Gpa, trying to hold on to every memory of Gma he could, despite the disease that was quickly stealing them away.

"Gpa," I said, pulling the photo out of the bag and handing it to him. "I have it."

He took it gently in his hands, and as if the photo itself pulled him away from the window, he held it in front of him as he walked to his bed and sat on the edge. *If only I could have gotten it back to him sooner,* I thought, *I could have saved him from ransacking the room like a pirate pillaging what already should have been his.*

But I hadn't. I'd been too damn slow. I'd taken too much time, and time wasn't something Gpa had the luxury to waste. Dr. Hannaway had told me he was entering the middle stages of Alzheimer's, but that he could still interact with the world, and that he should. She told me he needed to get out of his room and be with people more. I was trying, but he had no interest in the activities at Calypso.

Gpa looked up at me. He patted the space next to him and I sat down. Old Humper followed me and squeezed in between Gpa's legs. Gpa rubbed Old Humper's face, then hugged him with his knees. He put his arm around me, as if he wanted to cheer me up, but the almond slope of his eyelids looked heavier and sadder than usual. "I want to go home, Teddy."

"I know," I said, shaking my head. "I want you home too. It's not the same without you. But Mom says you're too sick. She says you can't."

"I am sick."

"No you're not." My voice cracked.

"I am, Teddy. It's awful. I know it. I can't hang on to things. Like this photo. How could I lose this photo?"

He trailed off. I swallowed the giant softball in my throat. "The photo wasn't lost," I told him.

He narrowed his eyes but didn't say anything to me.

"I was here last week. The frame . . ." I hesitated. "Well, it was broken, and so I took it to the shop to get fixed."

He pulled his arm away. He breathed deeply, then reached for my hand. "Teddy, I don't remember breaking the frame."

"It's not a big deal."

"It is."

"It isn't," I lied. Not telling him it had been another one of

13

his bad days. All the cleaning and calming I'd done to try to avoid having Julio and Frank come in.

"Come on," I continued. I squeezed his hand back. "Don't worry about it. That's nothing."

"No. No, it isn't nothing," he said. "I have this awful feeling that people are looking at me, as if they just spoke to me, just asked me a question, and I don't know the answer. I don't even know what question they asked." His face was red. "I don't want to lose everything. That's why I want to go home."

"I can't bring you home, Gpa. Mom won't allow it."

"Not here," he said softly. "Not your home. Mine. I want to be home in Ithaca, back where all my memories of her are. I want to be there before they're all gone."

I rubbed his back, but he glanced at me and his face softened. "Don't let me forget her. Please." I wasn't sure if he was talking to me or just thinking out loud now; his eyes were glassy and distant. "What I would give to walk down Mulberry again with her, and up the steps of St. Helen's, just like we did when we got married. Please don't let me forget her. Not her."

I held him and said I wouldn't let that happen. "I'm with you, Gpa. It's Teddy. I'm right here and I won't let that happen." I kept repeating that and holding him as we rocked gently on the corner of the bed.

He caught his breath and straightened, and I knew he was present with me in the moment. He grabbed my arm and held me tight. Those same blue eyes as my own stared back at me intensely. "I don't give a damn what happens or what it takes. Just don't let me forget her, Teddy."

"I won't."

"Promise me." He gripped me tighter, and I knew what a promise meant to Gpa.

"I promise."

"You are your word, Teddy."

"I know. I promise," I said, but the knot cinching tight in my gut told me I was telling him a lie, even though it was a truth I wanted to believe. It was the third time he'd asked, the third time I'd promised, and I really didn't know if he knew that or not. After the last time, I'd come up with the only solution I could think of, and I called it the Hendrix Family Book. I'd started taking notes, jotting down everything Gpa said and remembered. I wanted to get it all down, from beginning to end, all the little stories that, when woven together, made up the big story—especially his life with Gma, the story that mattered to him most. The HFB was all I could think of to try to preserve her for him.

The anchor of his life was buried in the ground, but with his mind cut loose, he drifted further and further away from her.

Gpa, the old war hero, had survived Vietnam, the long road home after the war, the backlash at home that he couldn't understand, my dad, his own son's, death, and his wife's death. But there, withering away in a room on the edge of the ocean, hiding from the world behind his veil of tears, Gpa was losing the battle against Alzheimer's.

"Let the disease kill me, Teddy, but don't let me forget her."

CHAPTER 2

CORRINA'S SONG

By the time Old Humper and I left Calypso Sunrise Suites, the sun had already begun to set, and we wandered down the boardwalk, past the skate park and through the crowds semicircled around street performers and art dealers, toward home. As we made our way past the grunts and the metal-on-metal clanging of Muscle Beach's outdoor gym, I saw Corrina underneath a stand of trees. With the beach becoming a rosy gold, the silhouettes of palm trees black stalks against the orange sky, I sat down against the trunk of one of them to listen.

She cradled one of those acoustic guitars you can plug in if you want, and she had one foot up on her amp, hair down in front of her face, as she played a slow, meandering, bluesy melody. No matter the song, she gave in to it, let herself go and the music come first. It wasn't theatrical, some fake-ass demonic possession that nobody buys anyway, it was like she joined the music, like something inside her danced along perfectly with each note. When she sang, her voice was warm and rich like the sunlight melting in the ocean behind her.

When she finished her song, the crowd clapped, and some threw coins and bills into her guitar case. She thanked people as they walked away. It was hot and her hair hung in sweaty strands. She wiped her brow and perched her sunglasses back on her head as a hairband. I couldn't understand how she wore black jeans and boots in that sun, and even in her loose checkered shirt with the ends tied in a knot by her belly button, aside from the sweat on her face, she looked cool.

I knew her from class. We went to the same mammoth high school up the hill from the beach, and although we were the same age, she had just graduated. We'd both taken the Poetry Workshop elective that spring, but even though I remembered so many of her poems so clearly, intimate ones about her being adopted in Guatemala by a white couple from LA, that didn't make us friends. We were just two people who recognized each other among a sea of thousands. So I didn't really know her, I just knew I loved listening to her sing, and when you're a junior in high school and your life feels like a whirlpool sucking you further and further down, and everything you thought you knew is cracking and falling apart and sinking with you, those little moments of beauty are the pockets of air that give you the energy to keep kicking up above it all.

She'd been busking on the boardwalk all summer, and since it was on my way home from Calypso, I often stopped and listened to her, adding and organizing notes in the HFB, or letting my own mind stretch as I scribbled lines of poetry. When I stopped to listen to her play, we usually nodded *what's up* to each other, or even said a few words, but I usually waited for her to notice me. But that day, *Oh, what the hell,* I thought. *Be brave.* I spoke up.

"You threw in a little extra nasty on those last riffs today," I said, hoping I'd used something close to the right lingo.

She looked at me and raised her eyebrows. "Hendrix," she said. "You crack me up, man." Everyone called me Teddy or Ted, but not Corrina. To Corrina, I was Hendrix. I liked that.

"Whatever. It was cool."

"Yeah, I've been listening to tons of Orianthi lately."

"Who?"

"Yeah. Exactly. If she were a dude, everybody would know her." She wiped sweat from her top lip. "Just check her out. She kicks ass." She looked around. The crowd had dispersed and we were left to ourselves. "But I've been working on something new of my own," she said. "Want to hear it?"

I nodded. She dragged the amp closer to the tree and turned it low. Her copper bracelet tattoo glowed in the setting sun as she loosened her hands and fingers, closed her eyes, and began to play.

Night fell over the boardwalk, and a mild intoxication swept through the people still scattered about, the drum circles on the beach got louder and rowdier, and fewer people stopped to listen to Corrina play. Clouds of marijuana drifted back from the beach. Corrina competed with the riot of voices that had replaced the boards and wheels slapping and rolling in the skate park.

As she began another song, a group of kids from school, most of them recently graduated like Corrina, wandered toward her. They were a roving pack of the ultracool, wearing their thousand-dollar outfits to make them look like ravaged, exhausted party people, either sun-stoned neo-hippies or dark-eyed, sleep-deprived hard rockers who looked like they lived only at night. They were the crowd I'd see Corrina with in the halls or out on the steps at school. Kids who jumped into each other's cars and shot off to parties I'd only imagined existed because I'd seen them in movies. On the boardwalk, they could have easily made a wide arc and steered clear of Corrina, but as soon as the guy at the front of the pack, Shawn Doogin, saw Corrina, he pulled them all over to her. He was impossible not to recognize. He was gigantic, and he stood there in his neon-bright sneakers and cutoff camo shorts, like he could have been one of the guys back there at Muscle Beach, doing military presses as easily as some people eat chocolate cake. He threw his arm around the shoulder of another guy and pointed to Corrina. They laughed, and then Shawn leaned back and shared his joke with the rest of the crowd.

Corrina played a song with a soft, sad chorus, the low notes on the guitar tolling slowly like a bell out deep in a harbor. It was one of her own songs, but Shawn and the other kids didn't care. They weren't there to listen. *"Our child doesn't act that way,"* Corrina sang.

"I bet!" Shawn shouted.

Corrina closed her eyes and pushed on with the song.

"Oh, we know!" Shawn's buddy followed.

They kept at it, heckling Corrina all the way to the end of the song, talking loudly, one of them occasionally laughing when he looked back at Corrina. A couple of the girls started saying things too, and this all surprised me because these were the people I'd always assumed were her friends, like Dakota, a white girl, one of the neo-hippies in a loose blouse and denim shorts who stepped forward from behind Shawn.

"Not going up to the O'Keefe party?" Dakota asked. "Miss your ride?" But even as she said it, she instantly blushed, red splotches burning an archipelago on her neck.

I thought Corrina might crank up the volume on her amp and blow them all away with some fat power chords that exploded straight out of hell, but she didn't. Instead she stopped playing altogether. She leaned the guitar against the amp and folded her hands over the head and the tuning knobs. "What are you talking about?" she asked, propping a heavy Doc Marten on the corner of her amp and waiting, staring Dakota down.

"Are you serious?" another girl said, coming to Dakota's defense. "You're not up there drooling all over Toby?"

"I'm not his girlfriend," Corrina said. "I don't keep tabs on where he is."

"Yeah," Dakota said. "You sure aren't."

"What about last week?" Shawn asked. "When you were in the backseat of his car?" He pumped and ground his hips and laughed.

"What?" Corrina said. Her foot slipped from the amp and she tried to right herself quickly.

"You think if you sleep with a guy, he'll go out with you?" Dakota said.

"I . . . What?" Corrina said, hesitating.

"He doesn't even like you, Corrina," Dakota added.

Corrina breathed heavily. "I didn't sleep with him," she said.

"Yeah, right," Shawn said.

"No," Corrina said.

"Oh my God!" Dakota shouted. She stepped forward and pointed at Corrina. "Yes you did. Just ask Toby. Since he's telling *everyone*."

"No, no," Corrina said. "D, that's not what happened. That's not how it happened."

"See!" Dakota said, looking back at her friends. "See, she even *admits* it!"

"No. D, seriously," Corrina pleaded. "Let me explain."

"Oh, Toby's explained it," Shawn said, waving his hand in the air, rallying laughs from a couple of the guys.

"Whatever," Dakota said, dismissing Shawn and Corrina both. "Here's the thing, Corrina. It's like you only hang out with guys now. Ever since you picked up that guitar and thought you were some kind of Latina Patti Smith."

Corrina straightened. "What?" she repeated, her voice sounding strained and weak. "Why would you say that?"

"Get over it. You think you're so cool? Well, that's probably why they all hang around you," Dakota continued. "It's obvious. You slut it up and they stick around."

"Oooohhh," Shawn said, egging Dakota on.

Corrina marched toward the group, her hands balled into tight fists. She headed straight for Dakota, but Shawn stepped in front of her. He was enormous, and he dwarfed the already-short Corrina. "Hey," he said. "Take it easy."

"Fuck out of my way, Shawn," Corrina said. She tried to step around him, but he gripped her arm in one of his bear-claw fists.

Whether the lights along the boardwalk were getting brighter, or the night was twisting and squeezing tighter around us, it felt like one of those moments where the heat of the mob rises and people start losing it: Corrina yelled at Dakota and girls shouted back at Corrina, and Shawn and some of the guys started laying into her too, and there was Corrina, still stuck in Shawn's grip, leaning right into the mouth of the mob and roaring back, and I got up, and I was sure Old Humper could feel my pulse whacking a hundred miles an hour in my veins and vibrating through my hands and right down the leash to his neck, because he started barking and bouncing around in tight circles, and some of the kids in the group looked over, but most of them didn't, and all I wanted to do was swat them up the beach to Santa Monica but Old Humper made the first move instead, and he shot forward, yanking the leash from my grip, toward Shawn.

And while most dogs might dive into a melee with their teeth bared, salivating for a fight, that was not Old Humper. He leapt onto Shawn's leg and began his very own slutty, eponymous deed.

"What the hell?" Shawn yelled.

Others screamed, because, naturally, they thought Old Humper was gnawing on Shawn's shin, but when they realized Old Humper's wet tongue was just panting along happily in the air, and that he had mistaken the brawl for an orgy, most of the kids started laughing.

Even Corrina was caught off-guard. She watched amazed as Old Humper went to town on Shawn. Shawn let go of her as he tried to free his leg, but she didn't chase down Dakota. "Looks like you finally found someone, Shawn," she said.

This got other people in the group laughing too, and Shawn looked like he might hit Corrina, but he was too busy with Old Humper. I didn't want him to punch her or Old Humper, so I dove in and tried to get ahold of the leash, and after a little dancing around in a circle with Shawn, I finally got a grip on Old Humper's collar and yanked him away.

Everybody looked at me, or at least it felt like it, and I didn't know if any of them knew me, or remembered me, but for a brief moment it seemed like everything had calmed down.

But then Shawn shouted, "What the fuck is wrong with your dog?" He couldn't stand still, and the current of fear probably still ripped through him because his hands and legs shook.

"Sorry, man," I said, glad I had a voice in my throat. "He's a lover, not a fighter."

Shawn didn't laugh at all. He swung so quickly I didn't have time to move. I'd been in five fights in my life and had won exactly zero of them, and when Shawn slammed me in the gut, I continued my perfect record of losses.

I crumpled to the ground and Old Humper growled and barked, but I collapsed with the leash wrapped tightly around my arm, so Old Humper leapt around uselessly, but before Shawn could do any more damage, Corrina called his name. He turned around. Her big black boot shot like an arrow and kicked him right in the balls. He fell to his knees. Everyone shouted at one another and Old Humper kept barking and I wanted to get the hell out of there, but Shawn had socked me square in the solar plexus and I wasn't sure I was ever going to breathe again—so I couldn't really move.

As I fought to regain my breath, everyone else kept yelling and eventually some of them dragged Shawn away, some of the girls calling Corrina a slut and other names as they left—names that all too often are thrown at girls and not boys who do the same damn thing. Why wasn't anyone calling Toby a slut? He was the one telling everyone.

Corrina remained and helped me to the curb by the trees. I sandwiched Old Humper between my legs, trying to calm him down, but he wasn't as dumb as he was horny, and I was sure he could feel my own explosive nervousness blasting out of me from the ends of my fingers as I dug into the beige folds of his neck and scratched.

"Shawn's a dick," she said. "But your dog is hilarious. Is he always like that?"

"Yes. Unfortunately. But I can't keep him at home or he'll ruin the furniture."

That got her to laugh again, and it came dancing out of her, free and easy. "Punched in the gut and still smiling," she said. "That says something about you. Also," she added, "cool band name: Punched in the Gut and Still Smiling."

"Thanks, by the way," I said.

"For saving you?"

"My hero." I smiled.

She laughed again. "Yes. Yes." She nodded, speaking as if an invisible audience huddled around us. "Yes, the boy is flirting. Punched in the Gut and Still Flirting—same band, years later, different bass player."

"What?"

"Never mind, Hendrix."

I still had trouble breathing, partly because of the punch, and also because I was sitting next to Corrina, the girl who set off explosions of nerves in my stomach whenever we spoke. A small, pale scar burst like a star by her left eye, and when she looked out of the corners of her eyes and smiled at me with a knowing kind of irony, she blew all the breath right out of me again.

She looked away, across the beach, and squinted into the dark distance. "But you know who I'd like to punch in the gut? Toby 'The Asshole' Fuller." She got up and paced in front of me. Her nostrils flared as she breathed, and I almost thought she was going to hit me, since Toby wasn't around.

"Corrina?" I said. "Are you okay?"

"Are you kidding? No. I'm not okay, Hendrix." She stopped moving and glared at me.

"I know," I said. "You look pissed."

"I'm not pissed!" she yelled. "This is what I look like when I'm sad, okay?"

"Okay," I said, as calmly as I could. "Okay. I'm not judging. I just wish there was something I could do to help."

"Ha. Yeah," she said. "You know what would help right now? A car. I wish I had a car. I'm so frigging pissed off, I want to go find that guy, right now." She kept pacing, swinging her hands in the air as she spoke, rapid-fire. "God! I wish I could use my parents' car right now." She made air quotes. "I've *eroded their trust* in me? Yeah, well, they can erode this," she said, flashing me her middle finger. She waved her hand above her head and spun toward the beach. "This isn't your problem, Hendrix. It's mine. You don't need to come." Then she quickly turned back to me. "But what about you? You don't have a car, do you?"

"No. Mom's? No, we can't use hers," I said. "Or, I can't."

"Why?" she asked, but I could already see her face brightening, an idea forming.

"I don't have my license."

Corrina laughed. "Hendrix, you are killing me. Who the hell are you, man? Who in LA doesn't have his license?"

"Me."

"Okay, but does she have a car *I* can drive?" Corrina asked.

This made me nervous as all hell, because (a) yes, she did have a car, the latest model of a little blue Volkswagen Beetle, and she was away so often she barely drove it, and it usually just sat in our driveway taunting the hell out of me, but also (b) I was not the kind of guy who blazed off into the night in my mother's car, because I was not the kind of guy who ever got out and did anything, but there was also (c), and frankly (c) was impossible to ignore. (C) was Corrina. I'd spent the entire spring trying to imagine a reason Corrina might press her lips up against mine, and with everything that Gpa had told me about how important his memories were to him, I realized I wouldn't have anything to look back on when I was his age, if I didn't get out there now and go make some of my own. I had to do something worth remembering. So I chose (d).

"Yes," I said. "She does."

CHAPTER 3

Escape from O'Keefe's

Half an hour later we were ripping up Centinela toward the 10 to find Toby. He was supposedly playing a gig at a house party in the hills. Corrina found some music on the XM, and as it blasted from the speakers, every twelfth breath or so I thought, *This must be what it's like to live like Corrina*, but the rest of the time I was worried we were going to smash into another car or a line of plastic trash barrels, or cross too quickly into the oncoming traffic, bust through the fence, and go crashing onto one of the rooftops down the slope on the other side of the street, because Corrina drove with gas pedal pressed to the floor, overtaking any car she could.

"Where are we going?" I yelled.

She didn't answer. We shot past the Santa Monica Airport and got up on the 10, and she drove even faster.

This was not my life. I was the type to sit at home alone in the semidarkness of the little bungalow reading poetry or contemplating the shifting shades of violet and blue on the walls as my eyes got adjusted to the night, and the silence of the empty house became a noise in my head. I wrote notes in the HFB so one day, there might be a record that the Hendrix family had actually existed, and that some of their story was a good one, because the one I otherwise knew, the one of the indigo-emptiness, of Mom's life away in hotel rooms on business trips, Gpa's exile to Calypso, and a Dead Dad whose face I only knew from the pictures I could find or steal from the old photo albums my mother left buried at the bottom of her closet, that life was beginning to feel lifeless, a non-presence, a whisper in a city of nearly four million people shouting.

But that night, as Corrina drove my mother's car faster than it had ever been driven, growling along with some band named Flyleaf on the radio, she'd swept me into her life.

We had the windows down and the air blasted my face. It felt good to shoot out into the city lights and scream a little.

"So what's the plan?" I yelled. "Another boot to the balls?"

"Nope. Got to scope it out first. A lot of people will be there."

She slowed when we got to the lush, dense neighborhood at the foot of the hills along Outpost Road. Somewhere, behind the trees and the hedges and the walls, were houses three times the size of mine, houses that looked like they needed teams of employees to take care of them.

"How do you know this place?" I asked.

"This promoter, Dougie O'Keefe? He throws parties all

the time. Bands play, people get wasted. People get lucky." She glanced over at me. "With contracts, I mean." We wound higher up the hill, turning onto one twisting road after another. "But I never got lucky here," she added.

Finally, the road ended in a wide cul-de-sac. Cars were parked everywhere, along the side of the road, in the dirt beyond, stacked two or three deep in the shadows beneath the trees on the slope up into the hill brush. Corrina found a spot up from the house. My heart hammered so hard I thought it was going to break bones in my chest, but I followed Corrina because as we walked toward Dougie O'Keefe's house, I kept telling myself that this was living, and I needed it, or at least, wasn't that what I'd always wanted?

O'Keefe's house was mostly dark and hidden by trees and weird, twisting rusty sculptures, but as we walked down the brick driveway toward the garage, one large halogen light sat half buried in the brush beside the driveway, a dull cone of light dimming and brightening, dimming and brightening, like one giant eye blinking up at the cavernous house set in the side of the hill. It was the first time Corrina had slowed down since we'd taken Mom's car. She looked from the garage to the balcony up above, both of which were packed with people. Hard-driving electric rock with folky accordions pulsed from somewhere deep within the house. Occasionally, the loopy, high-pitched voice of the male lead singer rose above the muddy music.

Corrina stepped close. "Okay," she said, looking up at me.

"Here's the deal. Just stay close to me and don't say much. Just follow my lead, okay?"

I nodded numbly. Not saying much was not going to be a problem. I was so nervous I felt like I'd slurped down a concrete milk shake and it had already dried and blocked up my throat.

Corrina patted my chest gently. "Just be cool and we'll be fine."

That was going to be much harder.

She looped her arm through mine and led me into the garage. A ring of tiny white lights ran around the ceiling, and there were no cars; instead there were couches and chairs scattered across the room, and people stood around smoking or lounging with limbs and whole bodies draped over the arms of the furniture. Corrina weaved us through the crowd slowly, squeezing us together and searching the faces in the room, but she didn't seem to know anybody. I didn't know anybody either, or at least I didn't recognize anybody, but there were plenty of kids my age there, and plenty of older people too. Age didn't seem to matter—everyone was a part of the same party.

We burrowed deeper into the house and walked up a set of narrow stairs to the living room above the garage. Half the room was floor-to-ceiling windows, but it was impossible to see through them because the room was packed with sweaty bodies writhing and twisting to the new song now playing over the speakers, amplifying the live music that was playing elsewhere in the house. Same band, same annoying accordion, and even more annoying voice, but it was a snaking river of a song with a weird husky whisper singing a druggie lullaby. Clouds of smoke circled the heads of the dancers, and I caught flashes of long beaded necklaces, gold and silver sequins, and shimmering black shirts and fishnets as Corrina pulled me through the dim room and its tissue-paper-and-wire towers of tobacco-stained light. Everything oozed cool, and I was glad of my hair coiling down over my eyes, so no one could see that I was terrified.

Corrina dragged me around a couch and its pile of worming bodies and paused by the black glass of one of the windows. She pointed outside to the porch that wrapped around the living room. Beyond, the lights of downtown LA were an upside-down sky of stars scattered over the valley.

"That's him," she said, pointing to a man in a crisp white suit and black T-shirt. A tinsel mustache and goatee bobbed around his mouth as he talked in pantomime through the glass.

"That's not Toby," I said.

"Hell, no." Corrina frowned. "That's Dougie O'Keefe. The man who has met me a dozen times and still believes I'm nobody. I gave that guy one of my demos, I heard him telling someone he liked it, and then when I saw him again, it was like I was Mrs. Freaking Invisible, and he looked right through me to the girls standing behind me and said, 'Okay, who's going to help me make her the next Iggy Azalea?'"

"Who?"

"Oh my God, Hendrix. You need an education." Corrina stared out at Dougie O'Keefe for a moment, her lips folding sadly. "I mean it. Like I wasn't even there. He just stared at these two super-tall, super-skinny white girls behind me." She turned away from the window. "Dumbest thing of all? One of those girls had freaking bright-blond cornrows."

She shook her head and moved toward the kitchen without me. I followed her, and she led me past a long counter that had been converted into a bar, where a man in a bright lavender shirt, completely unbuttoned, tossed bottles of liquor in the air over one shoulder, caught them on the other shoulder, and rolled them down his arm before pouring shots. Nobody clapped—as if everything he did was just commonplace.

In the hallway beyond the kitchen, there was a doorway to a set of stairs leading down to a room where the live music blasted. It was a kind of underground music bunker, because it wasn't until we were down there that I realized how loud the band was playing. I tried to tell Corrina that, but she couldn't hear anything, and she put her hand up between us because I kept dipping down too close to her ear. The room was too small for dancing, because there were too many people in it, and the little stage in the back was also too crowded with the keyboard, the drums, the two accordions, the bass, and the guitar, and all the musicians playing them, and the guy up in front of it all who looked like a tiny, skinny lumberjack with a mudswipe of a beard. He wore overalls

34

and a plaid shirt beneath it. He had dark hair gooped up into a fake bedhead, and it didn't move as he thrashed around and bucked like someone had punched him in the gut again and again.

I recognized him from school: Toby Fuller, eighteen and bound for CalArts in the fall.

He had the room whipped up in a tizzy of swinging hands and screaming, especially the two rows of girls packed in tight by the stage. It was obvious he was dancing for them, because when he stopped and rocked the microphone stand back and forth like a pendulum and the music slowed down and he quieted the crowd, he swept his eyes back and forth across the row of girls and whisper-sang to them. *"Forgive me and take it easy on me / all I ever said was I was a damn fine lover."* Then he threw his head back and yelled, "And that's what I am!" and the band jumped into its frenzied cataclysm of sound.

Corrina stood against the wall near the foot of the stairs with her arms wrapped tightly around her chest, staring at him. I could see why girls fell for him, the lumberjack-to-be springing around in his red Chuck Taylors. But when the song finished and he started talking into the microphone while the rest of the band tinkered with their instruments, getting ready for the next song, Corrina didn't press her way to the front, like I thought she was going to. Instead, she squeezed through to the side of the room where the sound board was. The guy who'd been there was talking to one of the girls up by the front of the stage, and Corrina hovered over the board, studying it for a moment or two, and then ran her hands over knobs and switches quickly. There was a loud shriek of feedback and then all the instruments went silent. The lights were still blazing on the stage and the guys in the band all started waving to the sound board. They couldn't see who was there, and before the engineer could get back, Corrina picked up the microphone that was plugged in over the board.

"Toby Fuller," she said into the microphone. "You're a liar." He stopped waving and stood stone-still, suddenly terrified, because what Corrina was saying was echoing from the speakers throughout the house. "You're a premature ejaculator! I know. Don't believe me, just ask him. He's telling everybody that we slept together!"

All the air seemed to get sucked out of the room and then there was laughter and people yelling, and the squirrely little sound engineer pushed his way back toward the board. Corrina tried to get out from behind it, but he got her by the arm and pulled her to him. She tripped. Her head pitched forward and hit the sound board. I jumped toward them, but since the place was a madhouse, I slammed into another guy by accident and his Solo cup splashed a pint of beer all over the equipment. There were a few electrical pops and hisses. The engineer let go of Corrina, and although she was unsteady, I pulled her toward me and led us back to the stairs. I pushed our way around some of the people coming down in a panic, but we were pinned against the wall briefly. We both looked back at Toby, who stood alone on the stage now, his hands at his sides, trying to squint into the crowd to find Corrina. He must have known it was her. It was impossible to forget her voice.

As soon as we could, we hurried up the stairs. A fat crescent of blood curled from Corrina's nose around the corner of her mouth, but I didn't think she even noticed. Once we were back on the main floor of the house and we saw the crowd unraveling in confusion like a herd loosed from their corral, Corrina slipped in front of me. She grabbed my hand and held me close to her, up against her back, as if I was hugging her, but really it was her making me hug her. We walked forward like a weird four-legged animal. "Come on, Hendrix," she said. "Keep me covered, but move it!"

And, as if she knew what was coming, I suddenly realized she was using me as her shield. Toby's voice shouted out over the crowd behind us. "Corrina? Corrina? Girl, where the hell are you?"

He kept shouting her name as we got closer and closer to the front door, and we were almost out onto the walkway when Corrina dipped under my armpit and shouted back, "I'm not just another nobody you can screw over and forget, Two-Seconds-and-You're-Done Toby Fuller!"

I couldn't help myself, and I turned around because I wanted to see the look on his face, and I was glad I did, because if I hadn't, I might not have known to duck, which I did, crouching over Corrina, too, as one beer bottle and then another went sailing by us, one hitting the doorframe and the other smashing on the hallway tile.

Corrina laughed. "You too, O'Keefe! Now you'll remember me—you old perv!"

Two-Second Toby threw another bottle and it hit the wall beside us. I pushed Corrina forward and we ran down the front walk, across the cul-de-sac, and up the dirty slope to the car on the street above. Corrina got the little blue car started, and with a swipe of blood smeared around her mouth and chin, she floored it up the road, winding away from O'Keefe's party and the roar of chaos swelling within it.

CHAPTER 4

EVERY NOBODY IS A SOMEBODY

Corrina wound circles through the hills at a frightening speed until I could convince her that no cars were following us and we'd gotten away. Eventually she slowed down, fiddled with the console, found a song she liked, and took a different road back toward the city. She bobbed along to the music as if it soothed her, but even the mellow tune and the warm breeze on my face couldn't calm me down.

"Can we pull over?" I asked.

Corrina threw me a heavy-lidded look of disgust.

"At least," I continued, "we should take care of that." Blood still dripped off her chin onto her T-shirt.

"Fine," she said, speeding up again. "I know a place."

She made an abrupt turn onto Mulholland Drive, twisted around the switchback road, and pulled into the dirt across the street from an iron fence. I'd never been there, but once Corrina cut the ignition and we sat there, catching our breath, listening to the gathering silence, I knew we were somewhere in the hills above the Hollywood Bowl. I found tissues in the glove compartment. She tipped the seat back, held a wad beneath her nose, and closed her eyes.

"Well, now I really am nobody," she said.

"What? That was amazing. You blindsided that guy so bad, he's probably still walking in circles trying to figure out his life."

"Ha. Don't make me laugh, Hendrix. I'm bleeding over here."

"Yeah. About that. You okay?"

"I will be."

She'd taken a quick and nasty hit, though. I wasn't much of an athlete, I sucked at kickball, for God's sake, but I was sure there were plenty of people who'd have called it quits after getting smashed in the face like that. Maybe it was the adrenaline that had kept her moving—or maybe it was something more.

"He's the one who's nobody now."

"Hendrix, no offense, but you have no clue."

She ignored me and kept her eyes shut, so I didn't bother her. I had no idea what she was thinking about, but if this evening had been any indication of what Corrina's life was like on a daily basis, I figured she needed at least twelve hours of sleep each night just to recover. My life was as exciting as mud drying in the grooves of your shoes, and in three hours with Corrina I'd had more fun than I'd had all year.

But her insistence that she was a "nobody" formed a dry

lump in my throat, because it made me think of Gpa. She kept calling herself that, *nobody, nobody,* as if she thought she was disappearing from the world, but it was Gpa who was the real nobody, because it was the opposite—he was more and more alone in a world quickly disappearing around him.

When Corrina's nose stopped bleeding, she pocketed the tissues and turned away from me, looking toward the trees and the specks of distant city glitter spotted among the thick pine branches like Christmas lights. "Hendrix," she eventually said. "You don't mind the silence, huh?"

"I'm used to it," I said. "It's kind of an everyday part of my life. I don't know if you remember, but there was this poem I read in class about what I called the Great Empty Blue?"

"I remember it," she said. She still had her back to me, one shoulder snuggled into the car seat, the other slowly rising and falling with her breath. She hesitated, then turned back, and looked at me with her sidelong glance that sucked all the breath out of me. "It was sad, and beautiful, but you totally stole the idea from Miles Davis."

I was stunned. I didn't even know she'd been listening to me in class. It made me feel like I was actually flesh and blood, not just a collection of thoughts, lost in the wind.

"Who?" I said, trying to hide my smile.

She laughed. "Hendrix, one good thing about you is that you are a terrible liar."

And she was right. About both things. I didn't know much about music at all, but Gpa had told me a story about Miles

41

Davis that had stuck with me. He told me Davis was a genius not only because he knew how to play and anticipate the perfect note, but because he also knew how to play silence, he knew how to let a silence ride and ride, making a tune rich and layered with the tension between sound and silence, and I'd thought that was something I should use when I was writing a poem about life at home, where I moved so often through the empty rooms, wondering what it would be like to have another person's voice with me. *How warm a voice can sound when it rises out of silence after you've waited and waited for it,* I'd written.

"Hendrix," Corrina said. "I liked it. I'm sorry I didn't say so at the time."

"That's okay," I said. No one had. Most of the kids in class made veiled, or not-so-veiled, hints about doing drugs or having sex, or at least boasted like they knew all about drugs or sex.

"You want to see something really beautiful, though?" she asked.

There was something I wanted to say but was too afraid to, and then I was more afraid that I looked afraid, since if I couldn't tell a lie, my face probably gave it all away.

So I said the first other thing I could think of. "Could you wipe the rest of the blood off your chin first? You look like a vampire."

She laughed and the whole car shook, or maybe just my stomach did, that ball of nerves exploding.

"Let's go," she said, opening the car door. "Don't be scared."

But then she turned around, flashed her finger-claws, and growled. "I'll only tear your throat out!" She slammed the door behind her and jogged across the street into the shadows by the iron fence. I took a deep breath and followed her.

The gate was locked, but we snuck down along the fence to a point where it dipped low and it was easy to climb over, and then crossed the dark parking lot to a short wooden staircase. There were already a few kids there, and although it didn't seem like any of them were people we knew or people who'd seen us at the party, we walked up the stairs, and then Corrina pulled me onto a dirt path and we snuck around some shrubs, away from everyone else, and soon we were sitting on the edge of a bluff, the wind in our faces, all alone and looking out over the valley. LA's lake of light stretched out below us and the spray of scattered stars above was its blue-white reflection. A river of taillights leaked from the city to the base of the hills, and I wanted it to go out because it seemed like it was all that was keeping us tied to the city—I wanted to believe we could drift off somewhere else entirely.

"Corrina," I said.

"Listen, Hendrix. Can we just sit in silence again for a while? I need that."

I nodded and gazed back out over the valley, trying to locate home, or Venice, or even the ocean, but it was all too far away. It wasn't like I'd never been out of LA—it had only been the year before when Gpa and I had spent plenty of weekends hiking up in the San Gabriel Mountains or even as far north as Sequoia National Park—but not really. My whole life I'd spent walking around beneath the haze of that valley, and now on the bluff with Corrina, that city of five hundred square miles seemed so small.

My whole life felt small. There was the wind, even the occasional lonely car horn calling out from a road in the hills behind us, but around that, in the vast invisible beyond the city, in the immense space between two stars, there was silence. I could shout as loud as I could from that hill and it would rise briefly but inevitably sink into the deep, unfathomable silence. Maybe that was beautiful too, though, not making a lot of noise in a small room, instead belting out one long, give-it-your-all yawp—music that matters because it knows the silence that surrounds it.

I wanted to ask Corrina what she thought, but her head was down between her knees, a curled, shadowed ball against a squat tree trunk, and she rocked gently forward and backward. I was close enough that I could hear her breathing through her nostrils.

"Corrina," I said. "Do you still want the silence?"

"Well, now you know I'm a disaster," she said down at the dirt. "I'm surprised you're still here."

"Of course I'm still here."

"Don't say it like that. Please. People leave when they can. Let's face it. People just get up and get the hell out as soon as they think they can."

She couldn't have known, but she sounded like a long-ago

echo of my own mother. Something Mom had said about Dead Dad, the nondad he was before he died, or at least, the nonhusband. Most often she didn't say much about him, or if she did, it was in that distant *I don't want to talk about it* way, but sometimes anger broke from her like water bursting through rock. "That deadbeat," she'd once snapped. "He left and then he died while he was gone. He could have at least said good-bye, since leaving was what he wanted to do."

"We promised each other," Corrina continued. "We weren't going to tell anybody." She swallowed hard. "It was Toby's idea, but I agreed. A secret. That's what I wanted too. Fine. We slept together, but it was supposed to stay a secret. That was the whole point. And then . . ." She trailed off. "You know what it feels like?" she continued. "Him telling everyone? Like everybody was standing around the car—watching. Asshole. It wasn't for them. It was supposed to be just for us."

"That's messed up."

"Yeah, and . . . it's so fucking typical. I should have known this would happen." She took a deep breath, and when she spoke again the words burned their way up and out of her. "Every time I trust someone they just get up and walk away. Every. Time. Why?"

Corrina lifted her head again, and I could see tear streaks stuck to her cheeks. She looked at me as if she'd opened a window in her chest and shown me the beating heart there, as if to say, *Please, please take good care of this, I don't want to do it alone.* But that look in her eye, the tremble in her lip, the wrinkle in her forehead all faded. She sniffled and wiped her face. She was hard again. It had only taken a moment. She'd turned right back into stone.

I put my hand on her shoulder. "Are you okay?"

"Uh, no, obviously. My life is a clusterfuck."

"So is mine."

"No, Hendrix," she said. "Not like mine. I feel like I'm in a prison, but not like I'm locked in a dungeon, something worse, like I'm free to go wherever I want, but there are still bars down between me and everyone else around me."

"But you're the freest person I've ever seen. It's like the rules don't apply to you. Like you just totally killed Toby."

"Yeah, but now I can never go back to O'Keefe's again. And that was my big connection, Hendrix. I can't go anywhere in this town. Believe me. People say *LA is so huge, it's so cool,* but it's just like every other town. It's small. Who you know is who you know, and who hates you hates you. That's everything."

"Come on. You're bigger than all that. You just graduated. You can do anything you want."

"Actually, no. I'm seventeen. My parents have me until I'm eighteen. They thought I was a genius when I was in kindergarten and they just bumped me up to second grade. But I wasn't. I just had parents who'd gotten me to read early. Turns out, I'm far from genius. Far."

"But, I don't know, you are able to get up and do things like no one else I know."

"Don't do that. I'm not magic. I roll around in the shit like everyone else." She got up and crossed in front of me to the far end of our dirt patch on the bluff. "You have to get out more," she continued, pointing to the city. "See the world and all that. Get out in it, you know? This town is wrecked. Everything's wrecked. School. The whole scene. It's wrecked. I need to get the hell out of here."

I got up. She stepped closer to me. I could tell she was trying to decide if she wanted to tell me more or not.

"They're sending me to Rosewood for a year of postgrad," she finally said. "School for the Emotionally Damaged? Yeah, that one."

"Can't you just go to college?"

"My dad, Mr. I Read Minds Like Professor X? He knows better. He knows what's best, he says. He's a psychologist, so there's that." She shook her head. "I saw my file. We got in this huge fight this morning, nothing new, but when he went out, I snuck into his office and I fricking took it. That's it— supposedly the entire *me* tucked into one thin, plain manila folder. It's still sitting in my guitar bag. My whole life stashed in my stupid guitar case. And *yes*," she said emphatically. "*Yes*, my goddamn father has a goddamn file for his own goddamn daughter." She walked away from me and looked back out over the valley. She balled her fists and yelled.

"I'm fucking out of here," she said when she'd finished. "I'm nobody here. I'm nobody to Toby, nobody to O'Keefe. I'm going. I can't stay here. I have to go." She nodded and repeated,

"I'm going. I'm just going." Her growing anger sent goose bumps spraying across my skin. "And to my dad, I'm just another diagnosis in a file. I'm not a file, Hendrix. I don't want to be someone's file."

As she stood there, catching her breath, staring out over the ripple of light in the city below, I couldn't help but think of Gpa staring out over the Pacific, fearing his disease was wiping him out too, making him and Gma nobodies, but they weren't, because every nobody is a somebody—a person with a story that proves he is alive.

"You're not nobody, Corrina," I said.

"Well, it doesn't matter what you say. I've made up my mind. I'm leaving."

"Where are you going?" I asked, but the gears were already turning, cogs catching, ideas rising.

"I don't know."

"How are you going to get to this nowhere?"

She paced as she spoke, swinging her arms out over the emptiness below us. There was a fierceness in her step, a magnetic and pulsing determination beneath her frustration. "I don't know. Train. Bus. I'm broke. I don't know. I'll hitchhike."

"That's a terrible idea."

"Don't try to stop me, Hendrix. I'm going."

"I won't. I mean the opposite. I mean, take me with you."

Corrina stopped and looked back me. She laughed. "What? No."

"I'm serious," I said. "Take me with you."

"You'd suck at hitchhiking."

"True. But guess what? So would you." I stepped closer to her and took a breath. "Take my mother's car."

"What?"

"She's gone. We've already taken it tonight. Take it again. She won't know until she's back."

Corrina raised her eyebrows.

"Take her car. Get the hell out of here. But I need you to take me with you."

She smiled, as if the many wheels of her mind were already spinning past that.

"I have an idea." I wasn't exactly sure I knew what I was doing—I just knew that I felt like I'd washed up onshore and Corrina and Gpa were there too, and we all had to get up and get somewhere together.

"Look, Hendrix. Don't go thinking you can save me. I don't need that."

"I'm not," I said. "It's the other way around. I need your help."

Maybe because I'm the world's biggest idiot, or because instead of being a mama's boy, I'm a Gpa's boy; or maybe because while most of the kids I knew wanted to get the hell away from family, I felt like I just wanted to hold on to what little was left of mine before it was gone—I couldn't help but think how this might be my only chance to help Gpa.

"I need to get to Ithaca, New York," I said.

49

"What?"

"We take my mother's car, and it's a two birds kinda thing, right? You get us to Ithaca, and I get you out of LA. You'll be on the other side of the country and you can go anywhere you want from there."

"Hendrix," Corrina said slowly. "Are you serious?"

"Yes," I said. "As serious as the Great Empty Blue."

Corrina nodded. Her own kind of mania rising in her smile.

"Anything else?"

"Yes," I said. "We have to take my grandfather."

She laughed and spun away from me. "We take your grandfather? That's hilarious." She looked back at me. "Oh my God. You're serious?"

"Yes."

Corrina walked toward me, and I could feel heat radiating off her. Maybe I had some too. She stopped right in front of me. "So you'll help me, if I'll help you? And that's it?"

"That's it."

"Fuck yeah." Corrina tapped me on the chest and then spun around and gazed out over LA. "Pack your bags tonight, Hendrix, because tomorrow we hit the road."

CHAPTER 5

THE GREAT EMPTY BLUE

I fell asleep that night repeating Corrina's words, "Tomorrow we hit the road," telling myself again and again that I was excited, but that was a lie because in the middle of the night, I woke from a nightmare that was more truth than any mantra I could ever repeat.

It's always the same: I'm floating on a small wooden raft, surrounded by water and darkness above, no moon, no stars, only the rise and fall of waves and the creaking of the wood in the water below me. A mucky stench follows me as I drift. Something lurks and waits for me. Rise and fall, rise and fall, the waves stretch and drop, and I can feel something swelling, a storm that gathers from the depths, not from above, until, like a whale breaching, the enormous shaggy head and shoulders of my father rise up and out of the water, as if he's climbing. Water and seaweed drip from his long hair and beard, his eyes like lightning in the night, he is ten times the size of any man, and I know he's there to smash my raft to splinters and pull me down into the deep gloom below. And just as the raft breaks and I sink with his gargantuan fingers locked around my ribs, squeezing the air from my chest—I awake.

I had fallen asleep in the living room, my bag as my pillow, and, as he so often was when I woke from this nightmare, Old Humper was there at my side, nuzzling me, licking the side of my face, reminding me I was still alive.

My house, the Great Empty Blue, with its dark-water-hued walls, was filled with the weight of Dead Dad's absence, which ruled and plagued our home like an angry god or a ghost. This was why I thought ghosts were real. Not the stupid cue-ball-covered sheet. Not the impossible-to-believe shimmering translucent image of a person. I mean the real thing: A ghost is an absence still present, the enormous weight still left when a person is gone. This ghost of Dead Dad hung about me everywhere, even in the spaces between words when Mom spoke, and he scared me most in those unanswered questions drifting in the silence of the Great Empty Blue.

I knew so little about my Dead Dad. All I really knew was how he died, far away from us, all the way back in Ithaca, where he was from. The drunk driver fishtailed it home in his own fog, while Dead Dad, alone, careened off a bridge into the black river, the car the coffin carrying his body, his heart carrying everything I wanted to know, down into the depths below.

I had questions for this Dead Dad—*Why'd you go? Why*

were you out there? Were you ever coming back?—but they were just whispers of smoke loose in the fog of his silence, because nobody would tell me anything. Not Mom. Not Gpa. "There's nothing to know," Mom would say. "He decided to leave and he left. He died when he did—that bastard." And Gpa said even less, even though, because he raised me, he was a father to me, which made me, in this depressing way, like another son to him. Or at least I felt that weight—the son who remained, the son who was alive. What was I supposed to do with that?

So after my heart eventually calmed and Old Humper curled up next to me, I fell back asleep, using my travel bag as my pillow, until I woke in the morning—and everything was different.

The sun swept through the front window, hitting the edges of the cut-glass panels in the cabinet like a constellation of stars lighting up the living room. The house hadn't felt this warm and yellow since Gpa had moved out. Even Old Humper could feel it. He lay on the floor with his eyes closed and stretched his legs and back. I scratched his head and then down under his chin and on the bridge of his nose, and then lay down next to him, and we remained like that, curled in the warmth of the sun, until I heard someone across the room say, "Good. You're up. Let's get moving."

I nearly had a heart attack because I knew it was Corrina right away, and I was worried I'd fallen asleep wearing only boxers, and that a morning missile was standing at attention, ready for takeoff, before the rest of me was, but luckily I had clothes on, and I'd been drowning in too much anxiety all night, so my body was in self-protection mode.

Corrina had dropped me off late, left the car in the driveway, and walked home while I packed, but I didn't realize she still had the keys until I noticed her swinging them around her finger. She sat in the pale white armchair by the window, and she looked ready for another concert, same boots and jeans, a new, clean, faded white T-shirt, and she wore a twilight-colored bandana to hold back her hair. She glared at me. "You ready?"

"I need a shower."

"Move it!"

Old Humper snapped to attention first and barked at her, happy for whatever was coming next, and I got into motion and made my way to the bathroom down the hall.

When I was done, I met Corrina in the living room again, where she stood by the mantel, holding a framed photo of Gpa in her hand. It was my favorite one of him, taken back in his Vietnam days. He's standing on a beach with other soldiers crowded around him. None of them are wearing shirts; they're all only in pants with the cuffs rolled up and their bare feet in the sand. They all hold plastic cups, probably filled with beer, and it's easy to see that the other men are all listening to Gpa. He's probably midstory when the shot is taken, most of the men aren't looking at the camera, but

Gpa is, he's looking directly into the lens. There's no fear on his face. He stares right out from the photograph with a strong, crystal-eyed confidence, as if he's saying, *I'm going to do whatever it takes to bring these boys home.* And yet, it was a war, and when you go to war, not everybody comes home.

But now it was my turn, and I had to bring him home.

"This him?" Corrina asked, holding the photo out to me.

"Yup. The War Hero."

"He looks pretty good here. Like, seriously good." She hooked a crooked grin. "How come you don't look like that? He must have been only a few years older than you."

"Thanks," I said. "He's twenty-seven in that photo, by the way."

"Still," she said. "You are related." She looked at me and cocked her head to the side. "No, actually I kind of see it."

"Yeah." I shrugged.

"Wow," she said. "But a silver fox, huh? He has those same Bombay Gin blue eyes as you do? Damn."

I shook my head. *Silver fox?* "I wonder if that's how he wants to be remembered," I said by way of distraction. "A man with a Solo cup on the beach."

"He looks calm." She stared at the photo as she spoke. "Imagine what's going on in the background. Maybe only a few miles away, in the hills, or upriver? It's terrifying. And yet he looks so calm," she repeated, pointing at Gpa.

"Remember that," I said. "Remember that image when we're driving with him. Please. Remember something sweet about him. It won't always be like that. You have to know that. He can be difficult."

"So can you."

"Thanks. But I'm serious. It's weird."

"I'm okay with weird," Corrina said, putting the photo back where she'd found it. "You're weird." She grinned. She glanced at the photo and back at me. "Sometimes you have the same smirk he has here, you know, like the right side of your face is a little happier than the left." She walked over and poked me in the chest. "Looks like you've got a little of your Gpa in you." She marched to the door and picked up her guitar case and bag. "Come on, Hendrix, let's go spring this war hero from his prison."

She left the front door open as she stepped outside, slinging the bag up on her shoulder, grinning wickedly up into the bright blue LA morning. I grabbed my bag and joined her.

"We're bringing him, too?" she said, pointing at Old Humper as I walked him to the car.

"I can't just leave him here alone for a week."

"No, I guess not." She tilted her head and stared at me silently for a moment. I couldn't see her eyes behind the dark circles of her sunglasses. "So let me get this straight," she finally said. "My great escape is becoming a little crowded."

"I come with baggage."

"Yeah, I see that. Basically the whole family, huh?"

"Basically," I said.

Of course, I felt a little bad for Mom, because she wouldn't understand why I needed to do this, and sometimes I felt that, after Dad died, a part of her had died too, and what was left of her attention she gave to her boardroom meetings and hotel conferences. Brenner, Stoddard & Pell Associates might as well have been her family.

"Does this car have a name?" Corrina asked.

"What?"

"A name, caveman, a name. Every car needs a name."

"Like a 2016 Beetle?"

"Oh my God, no! Like Emmy Lou, or Peggy Sue, or Proud Mary."

"Does it have to be a girl with two first names?"

"Yes. And preferably a reference to a song."

"I'm no good with songs."

"No you're not. Fine." She cocked her head and looked at the sky. "Blue Bomber," she said.

"Is that a girl's name?"

"Hell yes!" she said, jumping into the driver's seat.

I climbed in too and the light glinting off the bay window was so bright it almost hid the house behind it.

Corrina gunned the engine and rubbed the dashboard. "Okay, Blue Bomber. Let's do this."

CHAPTER 6

BUSTING OUT

When we got to Calypso, Corrina parked as close to the front door as possible. She turned the car off and sat with her hands on the wheel, staring straight across the lot, to the tall row of bushes and trees that marked the edge of Calypso's garden.

"What are you going to do?" she asked.

"Try to get him out of there with as few questions as possible."

"You can't sneak him out in a food cart? Hide him under a tablecloth?"

"Nope."

"Too bad," Corrina said, shaking her head. "That'd be pretty badass."

Of course I wanted to be more badass, but if Gpa was suddenly missing from Calypso, they'd have to report it, and if twenty-four hours passed and he hadn't turned up, the police would have to issue the Silver Alert, and we'd have every agency in the country looking for us, not to mention a very pissed-off Mom getting a blizzard of e-mails and texts and phone calls letting her know. None of that, clearly, was badass. If we were stopped somewhere in the Rockies, trapped, caught, knowing we'd failed before we'd even come down from the mountains, that wouldn't be badass at all.

I found Gpa sitting alone on the low stone wall by the edge of the patio behind the bistro, gazing out over the man-made pond with the chlorine-neon waterfall cascading over plaster rocks. The palm trees behind the rocks were real, but the air by the pond smelled rinsed with bleach. He was in his usual light pants and guayabera shirt, and he had his hand up over his eyes, shielding them from the sun.

"How you doing today, Gpa?"

"Another day in paradise."

I sat down beside him and gave him a hug. He put his arm around me.

"I need a favor, Gpa."

He waved his hand out over the paradise in front of us. "Oh, yeah," he said sarcastically. "Anything from my kingdom. Take it. It's yours."

"No, I'm serious, Gpa."

"Yeah, me too," he said. He forced a sad smile. "I used to take care of you all the time. Now look at us."

"Seems like a fair trade."

"Only from where you're standing, boy. It doesn't seem fair to me." He walked away to the far end of the patio. He pointed through the window to the bistro. "Look! The Gin

Rummy Club! Now, there's a reason to get out of bed!"

He laughed bitterly and I followed him to the side of the patio. "Well, can we talk about it more in your room?"

As soon as I heard myself make the mistake, he frowned. "It's an apartment, Teddy. If it's a goddamn room, it sounds like your mother has stuffed me in the hospital. It's an apartment. I'm not a patient. I'm a resident."

"Yes, I know. Your apartment."

"Don't you dare say you forgot."

"No, I didn't." I said. "But come on. Back to your apartment."

When we got there, I went straight to the medicine cabinet in the bathroom. "Already had the morning dose," he said. I ignored him as I emptied the cabinet into his leather shaving kit. He stood in the doorway and watched me as I grabbed his toothbrush and other toiletries and threw them and his medicines into the overnight bag he kept in the cupboard under the sink. "Am I going somewhere?" he asked.

"Yes," I said, but now came the hardest part. Lying to the Calypso staff was one thing, but lying to Gpa was another. I wouldn't.

"I'm taking you home."

He shook his head, and I walked past him into the bedroom. I found another bag and started filling it with clothes as fast as I could.

"No," he said. "Teddy, please. I know you miss me. I miss you, too. But your mother is right. I hate this place, but I can't live with you two. What happens when you leave and

60

go to college? She'll stick me right back in here."

"No, Gpa," I said. "I'm talking about home-home. I'm talking about Ithaca."

He came into the bedroom and sat down on the corner of the bed. "Stop. Stop, Teddy," he said softly.

"We're in a rush here, Gpa. Come on, please."

But as I kept at it, he grew louder. "Stop!" he shouted. I froze and looked at the front door of his apartment, because the last thing we needed was Julio and Frank coming to see what was the problem and Gpa making a fuss. "I'm confused," he said, more quietly again. "Please. What's going on?"

I dropped the bag, knelt by his feet, and held his hand. "Do you remember telling me you wanted to see Ithaca again? That you wanted to see your old church, see the old house? That you wanted to walk along the same old paths you used to walk with Grandma every day after dinner? Remember? Your church? St. Helen's? Where you stood with the priest."

"Father Ferraro."

"Yes!"

"With the bad breath."

"Yes! Father Ferraro with the bad breath, and you stood there with him, waiting, wondering if Gma was late or if she'd had second thoughts, because you were waiting there so long."

He smiled. "Her sister had brought the wrong shoes. The high heels. She didn't want to be taller than me in front of all those people. That's your grandmother, of course, always thinking of everyone else first."

"That's where we're going. I'm taking you there. But we have to get moving, Gpa. Please." I stood up and grabbed his shoulders. "Just stay with me, stay focused, and don't say anything to anybody on the way out. Corrina's waiting outside and we have to hurry."

"Who?"

"Corrina, my friend."

"Where'd you meet her? This *friend*." He rolled his eyes.

"I've told you."

"Well, tell me again, goddamnit!"

I'd told him all this before, but as he once quipped, the great thing about a person with Alzheimer's is that you can tell them the same joke over and over, because they'll never remember the punch line. He'd smiled when he'd told me that, but I hadn't. It was part of the awfulness of Alzheimer's. Once it starts, there's no going back, it proceeds with terrifying power, and it pulls you out of the narrative of your life one moment at a time until it makes you disappear altogether.

"Corrina's the girl from class. The one I see on the boardwalk some nights. We're only friends. Barely. Or, I don't know. Point is—she's way out of my league."

"*Way out of my league*. That's a silly way to think of another person. Don't put people on pedestals like that. What if I'd thought that about your grandmother? Look how it turned out. We were just right for each other."

"I know."

Gpa sat on the bed. "Ithaca," he said. "Are you really taking me home?"

"Not until you get your shoes on."

He glanced around the room. He looked relaxed, as if the knot of confusion usually cinched in his face had come undone. His shoes were on the floor beside him, but he remained motionless. "Come on," I urged him. He kept staring past me, so I put the shoes on for him, tied the laces. I stuffed his slippers in the bag and slung it up on my shoulder. I pulled him to his feet, and he followed me out into the hall. Then he paused.

"Wait." He turned and shuffled into his room.

"Gpa!"

He came back out to the hall holding the newly framed photo of Gma and baby Dead Dad. "She's coming with us," he said.

I nodded and began to walk him back toward reception so we could sign him out.

No one greeted us in the hall, and we got nearly all the way to the lobby before Gpa broke from his dreamy gaze.

"I was just thinking about the frozen custard stand," he said. "The one up on Meadow and Cascadilla. What was the name of that place?"

"Don't worry about it right now, Gpa. We'll figure it out later."

"We used to go there after dinner," he said, ignoring me. "What the hell is the name of that place? It's like *charity*, or it has a name that makes you think of church."

"Shhh. Stay with me here, Gpa."

He shook his head. "Finally," he said. "Home." He smiled like a child, but I wondered if he'd had that same expression as he'd boarded his final plane out of Saigon. A survivor's grin, a grin of gratitude, but shadowed with fear. Would it still look like home, if the custard shop was no longer there? Would it still be home? Could he call it that?

"Home!" he shouted when we were back in the hall.

"Please, Gpa," I whispered. "Don't make a big deal out of it."

"I'm going home!" he said again and again as we signed out.

I tried to look the receptionist in the eye. "Family reunion."

"Family reunion?" she asked.

"Yes."

She saw Gpa holding the photo and smiled. "It'll be good for him. You three have fun together."

"We will," I said, playing along all happy-faced, but feeling a little guilty on the inside because I knew she was thinking it'd be me, Mom, and Gpa hanging out less than two miles away at the Great Empty Blue—not the two of us flooring it across the country with Corrina. But the lie worked. She sent us along with a warm wave good-bye.

As I got Gpa down the stairs and into the parking lot, I humored him and talked more about the frozen custard stand that I'd never heard of but that was suddenly the most important half-eroded memory Gpa was trying to recall, and I hoped and hoped and hoped he wouldn't slip and suddenly think Gma Betty was going to be there waiting for him. If he went there in his mind, and I told him *No, she's dead*, he'd be in that weird limbo, that place like he was hearing about her death for the first time. A joke was a joke, but hearing about the death of someone you love again and again, hearing it each time with the pain of the first time—no one deserved that kind of torture.

But he didn't go there. And even better: what I saw ahead of me. Old Humper danced in front of the car. Corrina waved. She sat on the hood with her cell phone in one hand and the leash in the other. She leaned back, too, face bent up, the sun coming down and glowing in the twists of her dark hair and in her skin. A field of pinwheels whirred within me.

"This is my friend, Corrina," I said to Gpa.

She stuck out her hand and he took it, but I could see the wheels turning more slowly behind his eyes. I'd rushed him outside, I was introducing him to someone new. He turned back to the front door of Calypso. A flash of fear trembled in the folds of his cheeks, but he swallowed it.

"Your friend," he said quietly.

"We're just friends, Gpa," I said.

Corrina squinted at me. "Yeah. Of course," she said, and she was about to say more, but I held up my hand.

"My friend who's helping us get to Ithaca," I said to Gpa.

He nodded. "Ithaca."

Corrina got us out of there and back onto the 10, and when we started picking up speed, she scrolled through her phone and found a song she wanted. "Great road song!" she shouted

65

in the roar of wind coming in through the open windows. "A classic. The ex-hippies love it."

"Turn it down," I told her.

"Don't ruin it, Hendrix!" she shouted back.

But I was worried all the rushing and the commotion and the stimulus were going to send Gpa into a terrified fit any minute. I turned back to try to calm him, but he didn't need me. He was nodding his head slightly to the song—the urgent, charging rhythm guitar and drums, the lead guitar snaking low and deep, and grounding it all, a powerful woman's voice, as clear and heavy as a warm, polished stone. It *did* feel like a road song, something that surged and rolled, surged and rolled just like the Blue Bomber picking up speed as Corrina weaved it through light traffic on the highway.

"I know this song," Gpa said from the back.

"Yeah?" Corrina said. "'Somebody to Love'? Jefferson Airplane. *Surrealistic Pillow*, 1967."

Gpa sat up. "That's right. My God! 'Somebody to Love.' Exactly. That song. Betty loved that song."

"She did?" I said, looking back at him. He nodded and smiled. He stuck his finger in the air and wiggled it, just as the woman's voice cracked on a note and the lead guitar warbled through a short riff. A wave of relief swept over me.

He leaned forward and poked his head into the front seat.

"I know where I am," he said to me softly. "I know where we're going." He put his hand on my shoulder and smiled as we busted out of town with the sunlight in our eyes.

66

CHAPTER 7

FINDING THE MOOD RIGHT NOW

I had this soda-fizz feeling like I was going to puke while Corrina steered the Blue Bomber in a quick, fierce shot out of West LA, taking the 10 east, putting the sunlight at our backs and gliding through the easy midday traffic. But after we passed San Bernardino, Mt. Baldy, and Cedarpines and cut north toward Vegas, I felt a ridiculous burst of goofy energy, relieved we'd managed to get beyond the city limits, beyond the metropolitan ring, out into the dry desert hills, where the land opened up and the road bent east again into the vast, smogless, blue-sky expanse of the valley, because Corrina shouted into the dry, clear California air, "We did it! We're doing it, Hendrix!"

And the dam finally broke within me. "Yes!" I screamed.

"All right," Gpa said from the back. "I'm still here too. Try to get me there in one piece, okay?" He frowned and looked out the window toward the flatland around Victorville. "Where are we going, anyway?"

"What?" I glanced at him over my shoulder, because he'd been chatting with us the whole way so far and I didn't think he'd lost his sense of things.

"I know we're going to Ithaca, Teddy. I mean how are we getting there?"

I held up my phone. "Google Maps."

"No," Gpa said. "What route? How are we getting across the country? Which way are we going?"

The map on the phone was zoomed in, so all I knew was that we were heading west on the 15 until I was told otherwise. I zoomed out, checked the directions, looked at the two routes offered. One north, one south. The northern route was exactly thirty-three miles shorter, and it suggested it would take two hours less to drive than the southern route.

Corrina saw me fiddling and laughed. "Hendrix, the Great Navigator."

"Fine," I said. "We're going north. Next stop, Denver."

"That's the route I'd take," Gpa agreed. "I've taken it before."

The plan: We'd take the 15 through Vegas to the mountains of Utah where it met up with the 70, and then we'd take that rugged mountain highway to Denver, where we'd hitch up with the 76, drop down into the Nebraska farms and take the 80 clear across the enormous stretch of plains through Omaha and Des Moines, and brush the southern wash of Lake Michigan, and then cut straight beneath the hemline of the old Catcher's Mitt to Toledo, where we'd pick up the 90 to Cleveland and Erie and knife across New York State to those delicate little Finger Lakes via the 86 until we sailed safely into Ithaca, down there at the tip of Cayuga Lake.

As Gpa and I discussed all this, Corrina played with her phone, scrolling through it for music she liked. She'd listen to one song, then switch to another band, sometimes listen to only half a song, scroll to another. I began to worry she was paying attention to the music much more than the road.

"Hey," I said. "Let's just choose one and stick with it."

"Nope," Corrina shot back. "I gotta find something to fit the mood right now."

"What's the mood right now?"

"I don't know. But I'll know it when I hear it."

Eventually she found what she was looking for. Some band called the Electric Warts. They were an all-girl band originally from LA, but they'd moved out to New York. She knew one of the girls in the band. Aiko. The keyboardist. They'd met one night at the Dragonfly.

"They seriously rock," Corrina said, turning up the volume. "Not shredders, just old-school rockers. I love them. Edgy and doomy like Advaeta, but with this pop sound like Dum Dum Girls."

I stared at her blankly.

Corrina rolled her eyes. "One time," she explained, "Aiko brought me down to the Troubadour in the off-hours, which is cool, just an empty club and stage and the time and space to jam, but I didn't really expect to play. Except, when we got there, their guitarist was MIA, so they asked me to join! Can you believe it?"

Her face was lit up with the memory and she spoke so quickly and excitedly, even Gpa was listening to the story.

"So I play. Granted, not my own guitar, I'm better with my own, but still, I'm jamming with the Electric Warts, right?"

"Wow," I said. "I guess that would be pretty cool."

Corrina glanced at me with pitched eyebrows and a fake smile, because I obviously hadn't responded with enough enthusiasm. "I could have played all day, but then their guitarist eventually showed up and I had to let her take over. But later . . ." Corrina nodded along and smiled. The car picked up speed. "Later Aiko told me she thought I was awesome, like seriously awesome, like I could be in their band awesome!"

"Why didn't you join their band?" I asked.

"They moved to New York two weeks later. Just when you're about to get a break—poof. It's gone. Like always."

"Yeah," I said. We were quiet for a moment, and I was nervous I wasn't saying anything. "Well," I finally said. "Who wants to be in a band called the Electric Warts, anyway?"

Corrina pushed a big breath past her lips. "It never ceases to amaze me, Hendrix, that for a guy named Hendrix, you know shit-all about music."

"Shit-all, huh?" Gpa said from the backseat.

Corrina looked at him through the rearview. I turned to apologize for the language, but Gpa was smiling.

"If you ask me," he said, "this music is missing something."

"Oh, yeah?" Corrina said defensively. "What?"

"A good guitarist."

He smiled and leaned back in his seat, grabbing Old Humper by the scruff of the neck and scratching behind his ear. Corrina was about to say something, but instead, she blushed and stared straight ahead. She stayed silent but couldn't hide her smile, letting the Electric Warts fill the car with their loud, soulful, bad-guitar song.

About an hour later, as we entered Barstow, I noticed the sign for the In-N-Out Burger, and Corrina took the exit and wound us up the hill to the restaurant. We needed to stop, take our bio breaks, let Old Humper stretch his legs and do his business, hopefully keeping his porno discreet if he had to do it all, and get some food in our stomachs, because we were starving.

The parking lot was jammed with cars, and we realized it was probably the spot where everyone stopped in the drive from LA to Vegas, so we had to park far back behind it, near the faded pink wall behind an outlet mall.

I let Old Humper out first and he ran circles behind the car and then dashed off through the lot. Gpa stepped out of the car and called after him. I was glad. Gpa looked back over the Blue Bomber at Corrina, who was standing with her legs spread like a superhero and stretching her back from side to side. "Hey," Gpa called to her. "You're a great driver."

She stopped stretching. "I've always thought so." She took off her sunglasses and squinted at him. "But no one's ever told me so. Thank you."

"Well, someone needs to tell you. You know, I'm trying to remember the last time I was in a car." He turned to me. Old Humper had run back and I grabbed him by the collar. "Must have been with you, right?" Gpa said to me.

I fiddled with Old Humper's leash, avoiding Gpa's eyes, because I was annoyed with myself that I couldn't remember the exact last time I'd been in a car with him, especially when it was just the two of us, and that was what really sucked—I didn't know that the simplest moments could later become the most important ones. There was no way to predict. How many other important moments had I just let fly by?

Old Humper was behaving himself, so I asked Corrina if she'd stay by the car with him, walk him around a bit, try to keep him from chasing after legs, small children, or the base of the nearest lamppost, while I took Gpa inside to get us all some burgers and fries. She dug her guitar out first and slipped the leash around her boot. "He'll be fine until you get back," she said, tuning her guitar, and there was something so strange, seeing her leaning against the hatchback of Mom's car with Old Humper looking up at her, head cocked to the right, peacefully and lazily panting as she began to play. She looked relaxed, but I wondered how, or if, that was possible.

"Always with that guitar, isn't she?" Gpa asked as we walked toward the In-N-Out.

"I guess," I replied. There were people everywhere, in every seat, taking up every inch of table outside, so I tried to hurry him along.

He laughed. "Hey, slow down, Teddy." I did and he continued. "You're starting to look nervous. I know how you get."

"How I get?"

"Yes. I raised you. Think a grandfather can't read his grandson?"

I pushed through the glass doors and got us into the winding line in front of the cashiers. It was an In-N-Out large enough to service an army.

"You get nervous. It was like that on your way to school, when you had to talk to people in the grocery store, or at the movies. Anywhere. It just snuck up on you and suddenly you were nervous. I always worried about you." People had moved forward, the line was moving quickly, thankfully, but Gpa stood still as he spoke, holding up the line behind him that now went back to the double glass doors. "And then, later, when you were eleven or twelve, you couldn't take Skipper for his evening walk without that same look coming across your face. Poor boy."

I knew the face he meant. The smile that didn't have the energy to really rise, the furtive eyes; it was my pathetic attempt to disguise the horribly uncomfortable fear that spun like blurred fan blades inside me. Fine, we could talk about it. I was getting the look on my face, but not because I was embarrassed about being a little terrified twerp. If I looked scared, I wasn't. I was angry at him, because he was speaking too loudly and gesturing without thinking about how close people were to him, and he wasn't paying attention to the line moving.

"Come on, Gpa," I urged him, but he didn't move.

"I'm saying that if you like a girl, stop standing around with that trembling lip and just let her know."

"All right, fine. Just come on."

"You can't expect her to be a mind reader. You can't expect her to like you if you don't take a risk and tell her you like her. Sometimes a person just wants to know. It's that simple."

"We're friends. You don't know what you're talking about."

"Who knows what she thinks?" he said, throwing his hands up. "But you'll never know if you stay hidden in your own head!"

I took his hand and dragged him forward a couple of steps. He moved, only grudgingly. "Look, I know, I know. You can tell me all about it after we order the food. What do you want?" I asked, pointing up at the DayGlo sign. It was basically all the same: quantities of griddle-fried beef with or without cheese, and deep-fried potato. What was the choice, really? Just how much you thought you could pack down inside you? Still, I kept interrupting Gpa and asking him what he wanted, sounding way more pissed than I wanted to, until I realized I'd gone about this all the wrong way and a wild cloud passed behind his eyes—only a couple of hours into the trip and I'd already forgotten the care Gpa needed.

People glanced at us quickly and then away. Some continued to stare.

Gpa's voice grew louder. "You know, I'm trying to tell you a thing or two about girls and boys and what to do when you like someone, and you keep talking to me like I'm the kid. But damnit, I'm the adult here, Teddy."

"I know. I know. But keep it down."

"You're always dragging me around, telling me what to do."

"Gpa, please!"

"Everyone thinks I'm helpless, and I'm not helpless. I'm a goddamn vet. Sergeant. Marine Corps. Don't speak to me like I'm a child!"

The mother and father in front of us angled themselves between Gpa and their kids and placed their hands over their children's ears. A tall guy behind one of the registers glanced at us and quickly spoke into his black headset microphone. Everywhere in that packed zoo of a restaurant, people gazed at us as if we were crazy because Gpa was talking fiercely and quickly and loudly, and before the manager could come around to take our name and call the cops and get us locked away before we even got out of the state of California, I put up my hands and apologized to the crowd and tried to redirect Gpa out to the front patio.

"Don't apologize for me like I'm not even here!" he yelled as I maneuvered him through the double glass doors.

A year earlier, I would have been too weak and Gpa certainly would have been too strong for me to force him back out into the parking lot and away from all the people we'd just scared the shit out of. But I was taller and stronger and in the seven months he'd been at Calypso he had already shrunk—his shoulders stooped more, he'd lost weight. If he thought I looked worried earlier, I was really terrified now because I felt an awful sense of doom lurking somewhere nearby, like Gpa might lose it all together, and without a room to ransack, what would he destroy instead? Himself? And it'd all be my fault—and instead of preserving the stories of the HFB, I'd have ended them forever.

As we walked toward her, Corrina stopped playing and watched us. She quickly put her guitar in the backseat.

"I don't need to be treated like a child!" Gpa shouted as I angled him toward the Blue Bomber.

He glared at Corrina when he saw her, and she quickly handed me Old Humper's leash. "I'll go in," she said.

She was off in a second, and I put Old Humper in the backseat and shut the door, leaving the windows open. I had to keep a handle on one thing so I could focus on Gpa. He had at least quieted down, but he still muttered and eyed me suspiciously from the other side of the car. I hadn't been thinking of him. I knew what I'd done was wrong. I'd bludgeoned him with questions, bludgeoned him with stimulus, too—and for Gpa, we were already a long way from his quiet, calm routines at Calypso. Beyond the In-N-Out Burger, the highway bent up and disappeared behind a dusty hill. There was no telling what would happen a few miles down the road, but I felt responsible and scared.

When Corrina returned with the food, she placed it on the front hood of the car, the only part in the shade, and sat a few feet away from us, eyeing us closely as she ate her burger. Gpa stopped moving and leaned against the corner of the trunk, muttering and talking about how sick and tired he was of people whispering around him and babying him, but when he yelled at Corrina, "Who the hell are you, anyway?" without knowing what to do, I walked up to him slowly and put my hand on his shoulder. "Gpa, it's me, Teddy, and I want you to know I'm doing what you told me to do. I need your help, so please, please, please, please, please help me get you back to Ithaca."

Behind me, Corrina pulled her guitar out of the backseat, careful not to let Old Humper out, and leaned against the Blue Bomber's trunk beside Gpa.

"The damn music! Always with the music," he said to me. "I'm so sick of all that Sinatra and Sam Cooke and Ella Fitzgerald. It all sounds like they're trying to serenade me to my deathbed! Why do they all like that music so much?" He was talking about the dance mixers at Calypso. Yet another of the activities he refused to join there.

"But not this," Corrina said to him, her ear down to the strings. "I play this one for the ex-hippies all the time. They love it. Maybe you remember it? You said you liked Jefferson Airplane. Or, Betty did. Well, this one's for you and Betty."

She got comfortable and strummed a few chords while

I stood close by Gpa, not grabbing, only hovering close by, just in case. The old man still had fight in him, I could see it, but as Corrina began to play, he began to loosen up, relax his shoulders, and nod along. She played a few notes, gently strummed some more, and then hummed what must have been the first lines soft and low.

Gpa had to lean a little closer. "Wait. I know this one," he said. "What the hell is it called?"

Corrina continued to play and hum, louder but still gentle.

"I know it," Gpa said, a slight smile on his face. "Ha! When's the last time I heard this? My God, I remember hearing this for the first time on the radio on the front porch." Corrina paused and listened to him. "I heard it as I walked uphill from Woodcrest Avenue," he continued. "Betty was dancing by herself, singing along."

And on cue, Corrina sang out the first line of the song. She repeated the lines, singing them again, and then again, and then she played the guitar and let it crescendo and she looked Gpa in the eye and smiled and sang with open, wide-eyed warmth, nodding with her chin, encouraging him to join her.

It was loud, but not noisy, more stirring and uplifting, and Gpa bobbed his head. "Van Morrison," he said.

"What?"

"The name of the songwriter," he told me. "Van Morrison. 'Into the Mystic.' Betty loved this song. Everyone did. 1970?"

he asked Corrina, and she nodded back. He grinned and then sang along with Corrina in a scratchy, off-key voice. She smiled between lyrics as she sang and Gpa began to sing along more, intermittently, picking up a word here and there; they began to sing louder, together, and I put a hand on Gpa's back and he nodded, still singing.

Corrina let it go and go and probably played the extended version of the song, or her own version of the song, I didn't know, but I felt that weird, warm feeling when you put two and two together and realize something on your own, as I thought about all the times Gpa had skipped the sing-alongs and the dance mixers at Calypso, all because they were playing the wrong songs for him.

Corrina had found the right song for the mood right now. She knew it when she found it, or in this case, played it.

It wasn't right, being out there in the hot sun, a hundred miles or so into the middle of who knows what. It wasn't right, our plan, but it seemed like the right plan for right then. Because here was another story for the HFB, a story about Gpa and Gma loving rock 'n' roll—another chapter in their long love story. I'd never known that, and I liked imagining them dancing to the song on their front porch, clinging together, swooping around the wicker chair, pausing behind the burst of petunias to kiss. That was their Ithaca—and I had to get Gpa there.

CHAPTER 8

MR. AND MRS. FANTASY

"Oh, man, Yes," Corrina said to Gpa.

"Yes!" He laughed.

"What?" I asked.

"The name of the group," he said to me. He bobbed his head and Corrina turned it up on the speakers.

Gpa and Corrina sang along with "I've Seen All Good People" as it blasted from the speakers, but partway through the song, Corrina turned the volume down. She pointed ahead to a heart-shaped restaurant sign across the freeway. She'd slowed the Blue Bomber enough that we all got a good look at it. There was no restaurant anywhere, just the gray dirt, a few scattered sage bushes, a cloud-shadowed bluff way off in the distance. The red heart stood all alone in the desert, JENNY ROSE, the name stretched across it like a tattoo left behind long after the rest of the body was gone.

"Jenny Rose," Corrina said.

"Is that another car?" I asked.

"Uhhh," Corrina growled. "Sheryl Crow. *Tuesday Night Music Club.* 1993."

"What?"

"It was her debut album," Corrina continued. She picked up speed again, changed lanes, and pushed us ahead.

When the Yes song finished, she glanced back at Gpa, quickly scrolled to another song, and let it rip. "'Dear Mr. Fantasy,'" she said. "Traffic. Debut album. 1967. *Mr. Fantasy.*"

"'Dear Mr. Fantasy,'" Gpa said in the back. "My God. I remember that one."

"I had a feeling," Corrina said.

"How the hell do you know all this?" I asked her.

"The ex-hippies," she said. She glanced at me and shook her head. "I mean, they named me after a Bob Dylan song they loved, so there's that."

"And then what? They drilled you on oldies for the rest of your life?"

"Classic," Gpa said from the back.

"What?"

"Classic rock," he said. "Don't call it oldies."

"Yeah, Hendrix," Corrina teased. "It's classic." She laughed and then sang along with the song, her voice looping, harmonizing with the vocals coming out of the speakers.

Gpa nodded. "You have a hell of a voice," he said. Then he leaned back and looked out the window.

She smiled and kept singing, and even though we were in the car with the lifeless dust of the desert all around us,

I thought of her on the boardwalk, her voice rising up over the noise of nonsense, like that one bird hidden somewhere in the trees whose song makes you stop and appreciate the pause and the warmth of your breath within you.

"Okay," she said when the song was finished. "That does it. I'm making two playlists. One for your grandfather, and one for me. That's what we need. Every road trip needs badass playlists."

"What about me?" I asked her.

"What about you?"

"Don't I get a playlist?"

"You, Hendrix, might be a lost cause. Your Gpa, though? He's cool." She flashed him a peace sign and Gpa nodded back.

She fiddled with the phone. "And besides, you don't need your own playlist. Both of the playlists are for you, sort of." And there was something in the way she said that, maybe the way her nose crinkled when she said it, the self-mockery of her own annoyance at me, that sent ripples of happiness all through me.

"Fine," I said. I looked back at Gpa. "Hey, so Corrina's the Wikipedia of music. I get that. But how do you know all this stuff?"

Gpa smiled. "Your grandmother."

"What?"

"Your grandmother got me into rock 'n' roll. She was always a step ahead of me." He turned back to us and leaned forward. "But it was all because I had to go to Vietnam."

As Gpa began telling the story, I realized I'd never heard any of it before, so I grabbed the HFB from my bag at my feet and began recording everything he said as fast as I could.

THE STORY OF HOW GMA GOT GPA INTO ROCK 'N' ROLL

When people think of the Vietnam War, they assume most US soldiers there were drafted, but they're wrong. Two thirds of the US soldiers in that war volunteered. Gpa was one of them. It was 1966, he was twenty-six, and he was broke. The garage he'd run for the first three years of their marriage had finally gone belly-up. They had a two-year-old boy. They would have lost their home without her parents' help. He had no other options. He needed money and benefits. And so Gpa enlisted.

He had six weeks of basic training, and he went home once before he shipped out across the country and then across the Pacific. He'd only been gone six weeks and the separation already hurt. He could feel it—even in the records she played when he got back from basic.

"Listen," Gma told him when she sat him down on the steps of the front porch shortly before he had to walk downhill to the bus stop and roll out of town.

"Everything's changing. Everything. Except us."

They had a lot of the folk music she liked, and she'd played that Malvina Reynolds song about what have they done to the rain and the Joan Baez song "Saigon Bride" so many times after he'd enlisted he was sure she'd lost count, and he understood why she liked that wistful, sad, and almost innocent music, but in those two days between basic and shipping out, what he heard her play was different. Something he'd never heard before.

"This stuff sounds angry," he told her.

"It is," she said. "And I am too."

"Don't be mad at me," Gpa said. "Please. Not on my last day here."

"I'm not mad at you, Charlie. I'm mad for you. I'm angry for you." This was rock 'n' roll for her. She'd play it to think of him and why he was there and how she wanted him back. "Tell me you'll look for music like this while you're there, and tell me you'll think of me, angry for you at home." The song was "For What It's Worth," by Buffalo Springfield. "It's about some protest in LA," she told him. "But it makes me think of Vietnam."

And when he got there, and when opportunity allowed, and after he'd met other soldiers who were now listening to this kind of music too and who were getting it shipped to them, he heard the music go electric, he heard the darkness in the chords, and he grew angry at the distance and more determined than ever to do what it would take, as best he could, to stay alive and get home to her.

"So cool!" Corrina said when he finished, and in the hours that passed as we made our way across the rest of California, and I turned my notes from his oral story into a newly written chapter of the HFB, Corrina made fast friends with Gpa, talking about good rock versus shit rock, singing songs with him and finding others she didn't know, but he partially did, on her phone. I knew none of them. Sly and the Family Stone. "Me and Bobby McGee." The Lovin' Spoonful. Grace Slick. "Cloud Nine." "Eight Miles High." "Easy Wind." Thunderclap Newman. The Meters. Gpa and Corrina would say things back and forth so quickly I didn't know which was a song and which was a band. When Corrina found the song on her phone, sometimes I recognized a little of it. Maybe snippets from movies or commercials, but not as music I knew, because we'd always listened to the news at home or in the car, and I was that weirdo who went looking in old library catalogs online for recordings of Maya Angelou talking about how she knows why the caged bird sings, or Carl Sandburg reading about fog coming in on little cat feet.

But shortly after we crossed the border into Nevada, I interrupted them. "Hey," I said between songs. "Did she keep introducing you to music after the war too?"

"Of course," Gpa said. "I didn't want to get in her way. She loved it. Then I loved it because she did."

"So my father must have grown up listening to a lot of rock 'n' roll," I said. I didn't know why I'd asked. Or maybe I did. Maybe it was all that talk of home that got me thinking about Dead Dad. Maybe as Gpa had brought the photo along, I'd dragged the ghost of Dead Dad along too, or maybe he was chasing me, that wet hand rising out of the water, a voice calling me to join him.

Gpa was quiet for a moment. I looked back at him and he put his hand on my shoulder. "Yes," he said softly. I thought he was going to say more, but he turned and looked out the window.

"Like what?" I asked. "What were some of his favorites?"

"I don't know, Teddy," Gpa said. "I don't really know what he liked."

"Didn't he have records, though? What did he play?"

"I don't know, I told you," Gpa said. "Don't badger me."

It was a tricky line. Of course it wasn't right to badger Gpa, but it hurt, because I thought, especially now, that he did know more and he was holding back on purpose. He was my dad. *What was his favorite song? What was his favorite flavor of ice cream? What color was his Little League baseball jersey?* These stupid things mattered—they just did.

Vietnam must have still been on Gpa's mind, however, because as we crossed the border into Nevada, and Corrina turned up the volume when Creedence Clearwater Revival's

"Fortunate Son" came up on her playlist, instead of singing along this time, Gpa remained quiet. He stared out the window into the Mojave dust and kept one hand on Old Humper's head, rubbing at it aimlessly. "We're passing through Vegas," he finally said. "I want to stop and see the Raconteur."

I turned down the volume so I could hear him better.

"The who?" Corrina asked.

"The Raconteur," Gpa said. "We're driving right by him. I haven't seen him in years."

"We have to get as close to Denver as we can today," I said. "We shouldn't stop unless we have to."

"We can stop," Gpa said.

"Who's the Raconteur?" Corrina asked again.

I turned around in my seat to look at Gpa. "It's already late afternoon. We don't know where we're staying tonight."

"He'll find out we drove right by him. He will. He just knows things."

"No one is going to know we're driving by. No one is supposed to know, Gpa. That's the point!"

"Seriously," Corrina asked. "Who is this guy?"

"I'm worried about time," I said.

"*You're* worried about time," Gpa said. "You? We have time, Teddy." I could hear the anger rumbling deep within him. There was no need to let it explode all over again. The In-N-Out had been enough for one day. The incident had exhausted me and I probably could have gone to sleep instantly in the passenger seat, but I was afraid of what might happen as soon as I closed my eyes. I worried about what might happen when I did eventually have to go to sleep that night and in the days to come.

"Okay," I said, turning back around to face the road. I slumped down in the seat. "But just a short visit."

"Woo-hoo!" Corrina pumped her fist in the air. "Viva Las Vegas!"

CHAPTER 9

THE RACONTEUR

The Raconteur was the guy next to Gpa in the photo on the beach, the man standing tall and shirtless, broad shouldered, thick head of dark hair thrown back, laughing like he was howling at the moon. I'd never met him, but I'd heard stories, sad ones—the Raconteur had gotten smashed in the back after a grenade blast and had been paralyzed from the waist down. They'd stayed in touch, but Gpa hadn't seen him in years.

We were going to Vegas to see him, but not the Vegas Corrina imagined. It took us a while to find our way off the 15 and down into the streets of the city, keeping the glittering megahotels from the Strip to our left and behind us. Gpa remembered more and more, and finally, after we'd circled the Boulder Station Casino a few times, he remembered the beige, red-trimmed hotel that wished it was a set in a Wild West movie, if fifteen-story buildings had a place in old Westerns, and knew that the Raconteur lived nearby because he worked at Boulder Station and he wheeled himself there every day.

The houses in the neighborhood were all so much smaller than mine, some of them only trailers, or the size of one, with little squares of dust and dirt for front yards. The neighborhood was empty and desolate, which made me nervous. I wanted to get in and get out, because we had a road to stay on and too many miles to go.

As we curled around those depressed streets, the bent and twisted fences, missing slats and wires, I thought of all the times I'd complained about my house, thinking it was small, wishing I lived in one of the colorful, tree-shrouded mini-mansions on one of the nicer hills in Venice or back up behind the promenade in Santa Monica.

Eventually, after creeping along Avondale Avenue, Gpa pointed to another one of the houses, a faded pink rectangle. This one had a chain-link fence in perfect condition, though, and it sparkled in the blinding desert sun. "That's it," Gpa said. "That's where he lives."

It was a little past three thirty in the afternoon, and as we parked out front and turned off the ignition, we could feel the heat seeping into the car as soon as the AC shut off. I leashed Old Humper before I let him out and the four of us stood there in front of the gate.

"Are you sure?" Corrina asked. She fanned herself with her hand. "I'm a little worried whoever lives here is going to greet us with a gun." The air was heavy and anxious, and a distinct mechanical chugging and droning came from somewhere back behind the house. The two front windows and the glass on the front door all had shades drawn, and for a moment, one of them had its corner lifted, but it dropped closed as quickly as it had opened.

Old Humper paced back and forth, sniffing near the fence. "Well," Corrina said. "Let's see who's home."

As I stepped forward and reached for the gate, the front door opened and a man in a wheelchair waved his hand at me frantically. Old Humper barked. "Wait!" the man yelled, but it was too late. My finger had just grazed the latch on the gate when a shock jolted through me and left me feeling dazed and weird and tingly.

Everyone stepped back, and the man in the wheelchair leaned down outside the front door and flipped a switch in an electrical box on the stoop. "Okay!" He signaled us to come in, but I remained still, or sort of, as I thought I was swaying, and Gpa put his arm around me. He unlatched the gate and led us all in.

"Sorry about that," the Raconteur said. "Just a little some-thing to keep the neighborhood kids away. You get it bad?"

I shook my head, because what else are you supposed to do, cry? I had little tremors of volts still in me, but I told him I was fine.

He nodded, and then he stuck his hand out to Gpa. "Charlie! You didn't tell me you were coming. What the hell, man? Get in here."

He led us inside to the air-conditioning and closed the door quickly. His home was a warren webbed with wires crisscrossing the walls and leading to various keyboards and monitors and a scattered collection of computer parts and consoles and entertainment units that must have spanned four decades or so. There were Apple computers I didn't recognize, an old Nintendo console wedged between books on a low shelf, screens everywhere, including one on an oversized armchair and another tucked into a corner of the couch. An ancient Atari system perched on a stool, the game Pong still in it, rising from the console like an altarpiece. There was a big two-tone cartoon duck flapping slowly across one of the screens, and the Raconteur picked up a gray Nintendo gun and blasted the duck as he rolled past toward the far end of the living room where the carpet ended and the kitchen tiles began. He didn't have to go far. I was amazed how quickly and deftly he wheeled through the mess.

"Me, here," he said, gesturing to the room around him. "This is what I call the Nest. Welcome," he added to us. Then he frowned up at Gpa. "It's been how many years?"

Gpa glanced around and followed the Raconteur carefully. "I don't know," he said.

"Got to be at least four, maybe more. Jesus fuck!" The Raconteur shot a look back at me and Corrina and shrugged. "Sorry. My manners are all fucked up—I mean . . . Well, hell, you know what I mean. Sorry."

I'd frozen in the middle of the living room. Even Old

Humper was at attention. He was sniffing around the wires and computers, wary of another electric jolt. Or at least that was what I hoped he was doing, since I was still moving slowly and blinking and yawning and breathing deeply, just trying to make sure my body was working the way it should.

Corrina stepped around me. "Doesn't bother me," she said.

"No," the Raconteur said. "You look like the toughest one in the bunch."

"I am," she said, hoisting herself onto the counter that doubled as a bar. There were a couple of empty stools, but she ignored them. Perched like that, she was basically eye level with me, and she looked at me, smiling.

"I think she's right," Gpa said. He looked tired, and he slumped down onto one of the stools. "i'm too old."

"All right," the Raconteur said. "You didn't drive all the way out here to tell me that. What's going on? I'd say you brought the whole family," he said, but then looked up slyly at Gpa. "Except you didn't."

"My son's trying to help me," Gpa said, and I looked up from my daze to see what might be coming next, because I was worried he was going off the rails. I walked over to him and leaned up against the bar-counter between him and Corrina. He took his hat off and hooked it over his knee. "I mean, my grandson." He rubbed his face and looked up at the wall. The Raconteur had a black-and-gold marine Vietnam

93

vet baseball cap just like Gpa, hanging on a peg nailed to the wooden slats on the wall.

"And I thought I was the one with all the stories." The Raconteur smiled. "This calls for a drink." Judging from the collection of empty bottles in the barrel by the door, the Raconteur was a big fan of Basil Hayden's. He saw me looking. "Pricy bourbon for a guy on a pension, but like Abe Lincoln said, a man with no vices has few virtues. And hell, this is Vegas. Charlie, a glass of the good stuff?"

Gpa shook his head. "I can't."

The Raconteur frowned. "That fucker," he said, and we all knew he was referring to Gpa's disease.

"You two?" He pointed two fingers at us.

"Whatever you're having," Corrina said to him. The Raconteur laughed. She took off her sunglasses and hooked them on the neckline of my T-shirt, and I hesitated, saying nothing because I wasn't sure if it was the shock from the fence or the gentle brush of Corrina's fingers at the base of my neck that scattered little sparks of electricity inside me.

As the Raconteur wheeled over to his hutch to find some glasses, Gpa shook his head. "Lou," Gpa said. "They're kids."

The Raconteur looked back at him as he poured himself a short shot from a newly opened bottle. He knocked it back quickly and poured himself a fuller glass. "One more squeeze of the balls for you, isn't it?" he said. "Uncle Sam'll sign you up for a year, send you to the other end of the earth to have your back busted in a thousand different ways, and you can't even have a bourbon when you get home. Fucked up, isn't it?"

"Fucked up," Corrina echoed. She swung her legs back and forth under the counter, clearly enjoying everything that came out of the Raconteur's mouth. "Unfair, unjust, unloving," she continued.

"And not a damn thing we can do about it," the Raconteur said.

"Yup," she said. "Which all seems kind of lonely making."

He laughed. "Lonely making. I like that. Damn smart. Hey, you two an item?" he asked, waving his fingers at me. "A pair? Dating? What the hell do you call it these days?"

"No," Corrina said quickly.

"What's the matter with you?" he asked me.

"Uh, she has some say in the matter too," I said.

"Damn right," Corrina echoed.

"Yes. Yes, of course. I got that." This made him laugh again. "Well, I notice who isn't here with you." He sniffed. "The optimistic one in the family."

"Please," I said, stepping away from the bar top. "She doesn't know we're here."

The Raconteur nodded as he heard the force in my voice. "Look, kid, I understand. Your secret is safe with me." He added more to his glass and then wheeled around to where the television showed a few more silent ducks in the air, and a dog with the same shade of hair as Old Humper blinking back, waiting for something to happen. The Raconteur turned off the TV and repositioned himself in front of us. "Like I said," he continued. "Stories."

"All right, Lou," Gpa said. "I just wanted to stop in here to see how you're doing. You've got more shit in here than the last time." I liked when Gpa swore, despite what the folks at Calypso thought. It made him sound like he was trying to make a comeback, like he was holding on to something tightly and wouldn't let it slip away yet.

"Four years ago, five," the Raconteur said.

"I know. I've just had some troubles."

"I know," the Raconteur said. "I know." He wheeled up to the armchair and lifted the monitor to the floor. "Take a seat, Charlie. You look exhausted."

"I am. But I'm going home," Gpa said. "Driving out to Ithaca. That's the point." He sat down heavily in the chair and tilted his head back. "Finally."

"Oh," the Raconteur said. "Well, got to respect the road trip. Yup. Everybody respects the road trip."

"That's right," Gpa said. "Everybody respects the road trip." They nodded like they were referring to something from the past.

The Raconteur looked at me. "Look, bucko, your secret is safe with me, but"—he glanced to Gpa, who was looking a little droopy-eyed—"you need to tell me a little more about what's going on. I want to help. It's a long road."

"It is," I said. "But we have to make it."

The Raconteur frowned and shook a finger at me. "Don't

be a drip, nobody likes a drip. Strap on a pair and listen up. I want to tell you a story about your grandfather. Guy probably never told you about the time he saved half of us in the midst of a fucking shelling, right? If there's someone who can make it, it's that guy." He pointed to Gpa, who, while he might have been a war hero once, now was a small man in clothes that were too wrinkled, and who sank in a chair that was made for a man much larger than he was now. "Look," the Raconteur continued. "Make yourself comfortable. I probably have a can or four of the Beast in the back of the fridge. Find something to wet your whistle and hunker down. Grab one for your friend there too. She looks thirsty."

Gpa gave him a look.

"What? Tell me you weren't drinking beer at that age. Tell me it wasn't legal, for God's sake!"

"He's fifteen."

"Seventeen," I corrected.

"Still a kid," Gpa said to me.

"Ahh," the Raconteur said, waving off Gpa. "A year away from hell. Ignore the old man," he said to me. "Go find a couple of beers."

But he didn't tell us one story, he told us five or six and they all blended into each other, the horrors of being stationed up north on the high plateau near the DMZ in the first four months of 1968, how the boys all loved Gpa, how they loved that he didn't talk much, but that when he did, he was no bullshit, and how they loved that he was older than the other sergeants but still did every damn chore and tedious task with them, side by side in the mud and the reeds and the rain, so the most important word spoken between them was *we*, the Raconteur said.

And how we trudged through the stink of the wet ground, the smell of rotten leaves and branches, and gazed up at dinosaur-sized vegetation, the dinosaur sounds of the jungle, the muck and weirdness of it all, humping through ferns and trees dipping and curling with the weight of water like great green curtains that no one parted because the hush of death lay waiting behind them. Where are we? *We all wondered.* Where are we waiting or walking? Why here? *Rats in our bags. Snakes in our bags. Clouds and clouds and clouds of bugs in our eyes and clothes and hair.*

We never understood our orders or where we were going. Even when the destination was clear, like when the transport carried us north and landed without stopping, only slowing, and they asked us to roll right out into a field already riddled with tracer fire, bullets through the reeds and the grass, bullets through the leaves and the trees, bullets in the mud and in the ground. We crawled around with the whistle of mortars overhead.

We spent nights with our backs up against the sandbag walls in trenches, clutching our knees, screaming. We dug our foxholes and stationed ourselves there overnight, and we picked up activity with our infrared. Then the tonnage and tonnage of mortar rained down through the night, and the trenches were breached and overrun and a river of bodies in hand-to-hand combat. A grenade went off and we were thrown against the wall and the noise of the battle around, the screams, the yelling, the god-awful staccato fire of the AKs, the squelch of mud and the moaning all wove into one sound in our ears, and our hands were slick with our own blood as we called out for help, but we couldn't hear ourselves, because everything rang us into deafness and it was dark and we couldn't see through the pain, but Charlie dragged us out and into a deeper ditch and the fighting went on around us until the first light of morning, when all the wounded were brought out to wait for the helicopters, and we'd thought he'd waited there with us all night, but he hadn't, because he'd gone out and pulled down Jack Powers, Matt Washington, and others, too. There were fires in the villages, burning huts, burning shacks, trees and plants wet with fire, and God knows what else around us. Smoke in the mud. Smoke in the reeds. Smoke in the trees and the leaves. The war was in us, our bodies, our coffins holding nothing but the whispers of death in the breath of our bones. The jungle skulking our minds.

CHAPTER 10

ALL ROADS LEAD TO ST. LOUIS

When the Raconteur finished, he lifted the bottle of Basil Hayden's, eyed the level of liquid in it, hesitated, then poured another glass. "Hell of a time," he said before taking another sip. "God-awful hell."

Gpa had listened to the Raconteur's stories and nodded occasionally in agreement, but his face had stayed expressionless and somber. He'd remained still in his chair, only stooping to scratch the back of Old Humper's neck. But when I got back from a trip to the bathroom, the Raconteur sipped at his bourbon, and Gpa leaned forward, grumbling. "I don't know why that's the stuff I have to remember so clearly. There's all this other stuff I want to remember and I can't. Then there's stuff like that, and I'm sorry, Lou, but I want to forget it. I can still hear them, the bullets all around, clear as if they're out there now. You never lose that sense of being keyed up. Oh, Jesus, the bodies. I want to forget the bodies, Lou, but I can't."

"Well, I can't either," the Raconteur said. "And who can I talk to, who wants to hear about any of this who wasn't there with us? Everybody comes back from war having died a little. We're lucky it didn't get the whole of us."

"Oh, man," Corrina said. She leaned against me, just lightly. My hands were on the countertop. I leaned back against the bar and she simply placed one hand on mine and left it there. In my gut I felt a snap like a flag in the breeze as I felt the soft and sad breathing of Corrina's body next to mine.

"So many stories," the Raconteur said.

"They call you the Raconteur," I said to him. "How about one about Betty? For Gpa."

Gpa looked up at me and smiled. I think there were words in his mouth, but he left them there as he tried to control whatever else was in him. His eyes fluttered. Old Humper nudged him and rubbed his head against Gpa's leg. Gpa sat back in his chair and I knew he was savoring whatever other small memories he could piece together in the moment.

"It's true," the Raconteur said to Gpa. He wheeled one side of his chair back and forth as he lifted and adjusted himself in it. "You had someone to come home to. Someones."

And just like that, my father was in the room with us. There were Gpa and Betty and disaster averted, a family back together, despite the odds; and pulled right out of the past and into the living moment through story was Dead Dad, too. And I'm pretty sure this is what those ancient cultures mean when they talk about the power of story and the meaning of myth. This is what they mean when they talk about mythic time, when the past lives right there in the present.

"Did you know my father?" I asked.

"Not that well," Gpa said before the Raconteur answered. "I mean, who did? Right, Lou?"

The Raconteur looked at Gpa and then back at me.

There was a hush in the room, and like I was all too used to in the Great Empty Blue, the silence filled with the ghost of Dead Dad, drifting in like an invisible mist, reminding us he would not be forgotten—that he'd followed us on this trip too.

The Raconteur spoke first. "What are you hoping to find back east?" he asked.

"Betty," Gpa said.

I let that sit for a second, just to be sure he didn't say more, that he didn't go on and say something really strange, as if he thought, suddenly, that she was still there, and Dead Dad, too, that maybe he was twenty-nine again, traveling across the country, with another vet, their duffel bags tucked under their seats on the bus from San Francisco to New York, the long road home from the war after they'd survived Vietnam.

"Teddy's taking me home," Gpa continued.

"That's right," I said.

"And I have to drive the speed limit," Corrina said. "Which slows things down too." She picked up her can of beer, but it was empty. She took a sip from mine.

I rolled my eyes. "Yeah, and Gpa's registered. We're only

supposed to have him out for three days—including today."

The Raconteur pounded one fist in the other hand. "Damnit, you haven't gone through any tolls, have you?"

"No," Corrina said.

"Good," the Raconteur said. He spun past us, knocked back the rest of the glass of bourbon he'd left by the hutch, and began typing on one of the keyboards by the armchair near Gpa. "You sure?" he grumbled, not looking at us.

"Yup," Corrina said. "We didn't take those roads."

She still had my beer, and I wondered if I should take it back, but it seemed so natural in her hands, like she was all too used to sitting back easy against a bar top, talking about the road and places to go and how this giant world was meant to be lived in and roamed around and explored and seen and heard and smelled and touched and tasted.

Gpa looked over the Raconteur's shoulder at a small screen on the bookshelf. "You haven't changed," he said. "Same old conspiracy theorist."

"It's not a theory of conspiracy if it's actually happening, Charlie."

"Yeah, yeah. What do you have there?" Gpa said, leaning closer.

"Look," the Raconteur said. He pointed to the much larger screen he had placed on the floor beside the armchair, which was angled so that we could see it from the bar. "It's a map of all the major highways and interstates in the country where they have cameras reading your license plate."

"Seriously?" I asked.

"What the fuck?" Corrina said.

"Exactly," the Raconteur said. "This is real. Tollbooths are the easiest places, obviously, but they have cameras set up along many highways. Luckily, Uncle Sam can't get away with this without some of us paying attention."

"Which roads?" I asked. "All of them?"

"Can't know for sure, but you might as well assume them all, because so many of them do," the Raconteur said. "Depends on the state, of course. But forget Chicago and the whole state of New Jersey. Avoid them entirely."

"Chicago? That's our route."

"Forget it. Zap zone. They'll have your car and a picture of who's in it uploaded as soon as you get somewhere within a couple of miles outside of Peoria. Don't go there."

Corrina jumped off the counter and hunched down closer to the screen. "They're everywhere," she said.

"How do you know about the license plate trackers?" I asked.

"Look." The Raconteur wheeled around in a tight circle to face us. "Many of us do these rallies. Mostly motorcycles, but some of us have to drive cars or sit in sidecars. We do these rallies all through the desert, or the mountains, hitting town after town, just a little reminder that we're here. It's all perfectly legal, nothing to worry about, the cops are with us, this isn't 1968, no one gives a vet a hard time anymore, but a few guys had outstanding tickets, and here we are crossing state lines and we're at a rest stop outside of Denver and a couple of cops are shaking their heads, sticking notices on the windshields of a couple of the cars and one of the bikes, and they didn't even run the damn plates—they were just notified over their radios and given the plate numbers. The officers didn't want to do it, but they'd gotten the call so they couldn't ignore it."

The Raconteur tapped Corrina on the shoulder and she stood and got out of his way. He grabbed his bottle, poured more into his glass, slugged it, and slammed the bottle down on his leg. "Look, it's my job to make sure the servers don't crash at Boulder Station," he continued. "That's about all they want from me. But information isn't a little piece of paper in a dusty old cabinet anymore. It's an invisible thread of ones and zeros that extends infinitely into the ether. The information superhighway, they used to call it." He looked up at me. "That's a highway I can navigate quickly. I'm in a wheelchair, but I'm not blind. When I go places I'm not supposed to, I look closely." He paused and pointed at me. "You tell anyone, I'll make a new version of prairie oysters out of yours. You follow me?"

I did and I wouldn't and I nodded so he knew. "Well, there must be some roads that aren't tracked?" I asked.

"Of course." He wheeled back over to the keyboard. "Plenty, but you need to be aware."

"We can't go through Denver?" I said. "We were driving from here to Denver and straight across to Chicago."

The Raconteur enlarged the map and pointed at it with his hand still holding the empty glass. "You go south, through Flagstaff, follow the old spine of what used to be Route 66 and slowly bend north. You can't go the southern route because you'll get screwed when you're coming up north through DC, and it's taking you too far out of your way. This is your road."

I followed his finger as he dragged it across the screen. "All roads seem to lead us through St. Louis," I said.

"That's right," the Raconteur said. He looked at me. "You okay with that?"

"If it's the right route. Of course," I said.

The Raconteur looked at Gpa, who shook his head.

"What?" I said. "What's in St. Louis?"

"No, nothing," the Raconteur said. He looked away and waved his hand in the air beside his head. "I just get all caught up with things I remember from here and there. Please, ignore me."

"All right," Gpa said. "Enough."

The Raconteur began to wheel away, but I got up and stood in his path. "What's in St. Louis?"

"Lou," Gpa warned. "This isn't the time."

The awkward moment of silence began to fill the room. I could feel the sweat on my forehead. "Gpa," I said as calmly as I could. I didn't want to get him too agitated. "What aren't you telling me?" More silence. "Is this about my dad?"

Gpa looked away, clammed up like he always did when

I asked about Dead Dad, but the Raconteur raised his eyebrows at Gpa and gave it all away. I couldn't contain myself. "He died in a river outside of Ithaca!" I shouted. "That's all I know. But there's more to the story, isn't there? Gpa?"

The Raconteur looked back at Gpa. "There's no reason not to tell the boy that's where she lives," he said.

"Goddamnit, Lou!"

"He said it himself," the Raconteur said. "You're going through St. Louis no matter what."

"Who?" I said. "Who is *she*?"

"Lou." Gpa grabbed the Raconteur by the shoulder.

"It's the only way," the Raconteur said. He wheeled out of Gpa's grip and into the middle of the room. "And for God's sake, Charlie. He's not a boy anymore."

"I made a promise," Gpa said to him.

"Oh, go on, Charlie. Jesus, you're the one who doesn't change."

"I'm trying to teach the boy about promises. What they mean."

"I know," the Raconteur said. "I know you are."

"Listen," I said. "What are you talking about?"

"Ah, ask your grandfather," the Raconteur said. He wheeled past us around the bar and into the kitchen. He opened the fridge and pulled out his last can of the Beast.

"Goddamnit, Lou," Gpa said. "You don't ever know when to shut up, do you?"

The Raconteur looked down at the can of beer and then

tossed it to me across the kitchen. "Your father died in a car crash in Ithaca, yes—on his way to see the woman he was having an affair with. But she no longer lives in Ithaca, Teddy. She lives outside of St. Louis now. Small town called Troy, Illinois. You're going to drive right by her."

Gpa shook his head.

I took a deep breath as I realized how the story of my father's death existed in so many other minds, in so many other possible conversations. It sounds stupid, but for some reason I'd only thought of how it all related to me and Mom and Gpa, and it hadn't occurred to me that his name would be passed from person to person, that he hadn't slipped away into the great big nothingness entirely, rather that his name still existed on the lips of others, maybe not in the way he hoped, but there, alive in the present, a man who lived and breathed, and a man who'd obviously fucked up.

Gpa walked across the room, laid his hand on my shoulder, and looked at me through his wet eyes, as if he was about to say something, but he didn't. He leaned back against the bar. He put his arm around me again and I put mine around him. "My son was a smart boy," he said into the room, to no one in particular, staring more at the floor, or the space between Corrina and us. "But selfish." His voice wavered. "He sure was."

"He couldn't have been all bad," Corrina said. She smiled at Gpa. "Look where he came from." She was so much stronger than me. My throat felt dried out and wordless.

"No. No, he wasn't." Gpa shook his head.

He held on to me as his voice faded out, and I held him as tightly as I could. "Look," the Raconteur said behind us, from the kitchen. He was searching the cabinets, opening and closing them with a thud. "You know damn well the world is more complicated than that."

He was talking to Gpa, but I agreed. When my father died I'd been too young to have really known him. My memories were spotty and probably made up, little pieces of what I wanted him to be, more than what he actually was. But whether he was alive or dead, he was still my father, and there's a strange feeling when you're a kid and you know your parent is wrong. Not just wrong about some dumb fact you might have learned in school, like the faster way to memorize multiplication tables, but really wrong, wrong in some deep and fundamental way, like knowing the difference between a truth and a lie, and you, not he, know what's right. It made me think about my mom, too, and how betrayal, not only loneliness, had probably pushed her deep into the arms of Brenner, Stoddard & Pell. At one time, she was something else. Maybe she was more like a mother. Maybe she still was.

"Mom," I said out loud, as if to conjure her into the space too.

Gpa hung heavy on me now, and I walked him back to the armchair. Corrina helped me get him into the chair. "I'm tired," he said.

"Yeah," Corrina said. "And we should eat."

The Raconteur seemed to find what he was looking for in the cupboards, and he wheeled back into the room holding a glass with a drink that had a slice of lime in it. "Pizza?" he asked. His eyes were bloodshot.

"Yes," Corrina said. "And make me one of whatever you're having. I don't think we're going anywhere."

She was right. Gpa already looked distant and half asleep or disoriented in the chair, and the sunlight that had once crept around the corners of the shades was now gone. I peeked out one window and saw that it was already night. There was no point in driving now anyway, because we had a new route.

CHAPTER 11

WHERE WE'RE FROM

There were more war stories, and then Gpa fell asleep in the chair and the Raconteur fell asleep in his, and Old Humper remained curled up at Gpa's feet, but Corrina and I were wide awake. "Want to see if we can find our way to the roof?" she asked.

We unlocked the back door in the kitchen and found the shed attached to the house that must have contained the Raconteur's generator. We climbed up and hoisted ourselves onto the Raconteur's flat roof. We walked over to the front and hung our feet over the edge. Across the street, the Raconteur's neighbors had built a wall out of cinder blocks around their yard, but from the roof, we could see over it, and it contained a small primary-colored plastic jungle gym and slide.

"It's weird," Corrina said pointing to it. "Thinking about growing up somewhere else. Imagine if you grew up here."

"I'd have been a cowboy, riding into the hills at sunrise and back just after sunset," I said, pointing to the shadowy blue-and-purple mountains in the distance. I knew they were miles and miles away, but they seemed right there, as if they rose out of the ground at the other end of the neighborhood.

"Yeah," she said. "Me too." She was quiet for a moment. "I think about what it would be like to grow up somewhere else. Who would I be if the ex-hippies never took me out of Guatemala?"

"You probably wouldn't know the Electric Warts."

She laughed a small, soft laugh. It had been too damn hot earlier, so I'd left my denim jacket in the Blue Bomber, but now that the sun had gone down the desert air was much cooler. Corrina was cold too. She shivered. I wished I had my jacket so I could have thrown it over her shoulders.

"You'd be a totally different person," I said.

"Would that be a good thing or a bad thing?" she asked.

"I don't know," I said. "But I wouldn't know you. You wouldn't be you. And that would suck for me."

She shrugged.

"But it's not what you're asking."

"No." She paused and then continued. "I feel like my whole life I hear people telling me who I am *not*. I feel all the things I'm not, or not totally a part of. I just want to feel a part of something. I just want to be something I am. Fully."

I thought she might say more, but she didn't. Instead, we were quiet for a while, and we looked out over the neighborhood of dark or barely lit rectangles. But I knew Corrina was watching me, too. "I come from a weird home," I eventually said. "I mean, I always guessed Dead Dad was screwing around behind Mom's back, but she's a little fucked up to not tell me more about it. For knowing, and not saying anything to me. All that silence is just as bad as a lie."

"I get that," Corrina said, leaning back. "I really get that."

I was feeling strange, because having been electrocuted will do that, but also because I was still thinking about Dead Dad and the woman in St. Louis, and Mom and what she knew or didn't, and why Gpa couldn't talk about it either, and why this kind of stuff that really is the most important is always the stuff no one wants to talk about.

"We both have weird families," I finally said, just to say something, to try at least.

"Yeah, kind of." She sniffed. "We both don't know a lot about our parents."

"Your parents don't have any mysteries, though," I said.

"I'm not talking about the ex-hippies," she said. "My *biological* parents. Even that word hides them. *Biological:* like they're lost and locked away in some book or encyclopedia. Where are they? Who are they? You know. Those kinds of mysteries."

"I'm sorry," I said. "Yeah."

"And then . . ." She looked at me and then away, out toward the mountains. "That all leads to other mysteries. Mysteries—more like black holes of understanding. Like I'm just stuck between two different worlds all the time, but I don't really understand either of the two worlds I'm stuck between. I sometimes feel like people want me to choose one of the worlds, but I can't. I'm right in the middle, and nobody can figure that out. Why do I have to figure it all out?"

I nodded. "That feels lonely."

"Fuck yeah it does." Corrina shook her head. "So I've got these parents who love me, yeah yeah yeah, but they don't know me. I mean, my dad can tell you a concert, name the date, the year, who was onstage, the set list. But he doesn't play an instrument. So what does he really know? I always think about that. Did my parents in Guatemala play an instrument?"

"You wonder if that's why you play? Genetics and all that?"

"Yes and no," Corrina said. She put both hands to her head as if she was keeping it from splitting open. "It's not that simple. It's from the ex-hippies to some extent. They're the ones who let me sign up for Girls Rock Camp. I went for years. That's where I starting learning the songs they love. It's so weird. They were skeptical, but once they heard me playing the stuff they love, they were okay with it."

She got up and walked across the roof and stood by the other edge with her hands in her pockets, staring toward the glow of the Vegas skyline, the single spire of gray light rising from the pyramid and the candy-colored haze of buildings around it. It might have looked like LA, except that it was nothing but hotels.

Corrina kept her back to me as she continued. "Sometimes I wonder if I play because it was the only time they listened to me. I mean really looked at me and really listened to me. The only time they were really proud, or at least the only time I could see it on their faces. But I was playing their music, you know? And I am their world. I am. But I'm also not, and they never talk about that."

I was about to say, "Yeah, I know," but then I didn't. I stayed silent and just listened. Because I didn't really know, and it would have been stupid of me to think I did.

"My dad makes these lists of my behavior patterns, but never says, *Hey, how does it feel to be a brown girl raised by white parents?* And my mom? *Honey, we don't see race,* she says. *We only see family.*" Corrina turned to me, and even in the dimness I could see her eyes glisten with a few tears. "That's fucked up, Hendrix. It just is. Like, if you don't see race, you don't see *me*, Mom." She gestured to the space between us. "If I'm across the room from them at a party, no one looks at my parents and just assumes they're my parents. They look around for brown folks."

I thought about the photo Corrina had found back at the Great Empty Blue, the photo of Gpa, the old war hero with the Solo cup. She'd teased me, but beneath it, she was saying, *This is your history, Hendrix.* It was right there, looking me in the eyes. It reminded me of Mrs. Keene's first assignment in poetry class: the "Where I'm From" poems. She'd asked us all to read our poems out loud, and Corrina's was about a swirling ball of fire, something like the sun, with sunspots leaping out and diving back into the smoldering center.

"Now, Corrina," Mrs. Keene had said to her in front of the whole class. "What I asked you to do was write specifics, not abstractions. Talk about where you're from, the food, the culture, the smells of your grandmother's cooking, and all that, the sounds of the neighborhood."

Corrina stood back up. "Fine," she said. "'Where I'm From.' Whiskey and mashed potatoes. My parents are fucking Irish."

Corrina had been booted from class for her language.

But how could I blame her for her frustration? Words like *home* and *family* didn't need to fit in a tidy little box with a label on the front so it could conveniently fit on someone else's shelf. What if Corrina started her own family book? The CFB. What would that look like? What did family mean, exactly? And what was home, for that matter? It sure as hell didn't have to be my abyss of the Great Empty Blue.

On the roof, Corrina's voice had gone hoarse. "Why am I even telling you all this? I must sound insane. Maybe my dad's right?"

"Hey," I said moving a little closer to her. "You're not crazy."

"Yeah, right. You don't know me, white boy."

"No, I'm not saying that. I'm just saying that I'm listening and you don't sound crazy to me." I took a deep breath. "For real. I remember your poem from class about the swirling ball of fire. It made sense to me. It was awesome. Vivid, just like a frigging ball of fire should be! It all made sense to me."

"It did?"

"Like it was something alive and fluid—something on the move, maybe." I paused. "I should have said something to you then."

Corrina sniffed.

I walked over to her and looked out toward the skyline. "I should have. And I should have said something to Mrs. Keene, too."

Corrina took a deep breath through her nose. "Not going to lie, Hendrix, would have been nice if someone else had told her that."

I nodded and we stood there, side by side, staring at the gaudy skyline, for a while. "Okay," I eventually said. I pointed to the city. "So that's Vegas. But we're going elsewhere." I steered us around to the other side of the roof so we were looking toward the blue-shadowed mountains in the distance. "I don't know what's out there," I said, pointing to the invisibleness behind the peaks.

"But we're going anyway," Corrina said. "Story of my life. Every day I feel like I get up and jump off a cliff, hoping there's water below."

"Or fire," I said. "A solar flare leaping off the surface of the sun, hoping to fall back into the fire, not fizzle out—it was something like that, right?"

Corrina nodded. "Something like that. Man, I can't believe you remember all that."

"I remember all kinds of lines from poems. It's like . . . *my thing.*"

"Like what else?"

I paused, because I realized that my hand was only inches from hers, and, to me at least, there was this crazy invisible fire leaping back and forth between us, like it was rising off our skin and fusing in the soft breath of space between her fingers and mine, and one voice inside me told me to grab her hand and another told me to cool it, because she'd just poured her guts out to me, and what I would have given for a frigging instruction manual to follow, but I had nothing, so instead I stammered and twitched as I just tried to say the first thing that came to mind.

"Do you know E. E. Cummings?" I said.

"I'm sorry about his name."

"Ha. And ha. The thing is, he has this poem and it reminds me of you: (*the voice of your eyes is deeper than all roses*) / *nobody, not even the rain, has such small hands*."

She looked at me and smiled. "*Voice of your eyes*, I like that."

"I like your hands," I said, and then I took one of hers and pressed it to mine, palm to palm, heat to heat, my giant, trembling fingers standing up over hers. "They're so much smaller. But I think they're stronger."

"From playing guitar."

"Yeah, but also just from you. You're strong."

"So are you."

She leaned into me, face into my chest, and I wrapped my arms around her gently. I felt her breath through my shirt. "Just look at us," she mumbled. "Who'd have ever guessed we'd be standing on a roof in Vegas together."

We stayed like that for a while, wrapped up in each other's

arms, wrapped up in each other's silence, letting it hold us until it became a kind of cocoon of warmth that kept the cool air away.

Eventually we sat down and looked at the mountains and I smiled as she began to sing with a voice as beautiful as the desert light, the colors of twilight sinking into night, the color of that bottom-drop feeling that fell through my gut when she sat on the edge of the roof, leaned against my shoulder, and sang.

She said it was one Gpa might like, called "Bell Bottom Blues," but I thought it meant something very different to her, something private, something that resonated deep within her, and the great thing about music, as I had begun to learn, was that it moves like a spirit or a spell, powerful and independent, within each of us, and as she sang, my mind drifted and I wondered if Gpa had heard the song back in his old war hero days and liked it, and if he sang those words to himself, "I don't want to fade away," when he was on the other side of the world in Vietnam, and if Gma had heard to it too while she waited and waited and waited for him to come home.

"Sing one of yours," I said when she finished. "Those are my favorites."

Corrina nodded. She didn't look at me. She sat quiet for a moment and I could hear her, feel her, catching her breath. "Okay," she said.

CHAPTER 12

WHERE WE'RE GOING

Corrina and I both slept in the living room with Gpa, her on the couch, me on the floor, in case Gpa got up and was confused, but he wasn't the first one up. The Raconteur woke up before all of us and made his way into the kitchen to make coffee. Old Humper followed him, and being Old Humper, must have gone after the water cooler by the bathroom door, because I woke to a crash in the kitchen and the Raconteur shouting, and before I could get up and really collect my thoughts, I heard the back door in the kitchen slam.

There was more moaning and groaning from the kitchen, but I rubbed my face and turned to Gpa, who was looking around skeptically. "Gpa," I said. "It's me, Teddy. We fell asleep in the living room." He squinted at me and rolled his stiff shoulders. He stood uneasily and inspected the room.

"That fucking dog!" the Raconteur yelled from the kitchen. "Get in here and clean up his mess!"

Gpa glanced from me, to the kitchen, to Corrina on the

couch, and back to the kitchen, deep lines of worry wrinkling his face. I got up and hugged him and reminded him that we were on a road trip together and that we were heading back to Ithaca and that we'd fallen asleep at the Raconteur's. I told him all of this as slowly and simply as I could while the Raconteur continued to shout behind me.

"Everybody heard you the first time," Corrina told the Raconteur as she rolled off the couch. She pulled a dish towel from the fridge handle and wiped up the spilled water.

We cleaned ourselves up after that, ate a few bowls of cereal, fed Old Humper, and thanked the Raconteur for his hospitality.

The Raconteur wheeled onto his small stoop and cut the current from the fence so I didn't go round two of stupidly electrocuting myself, and when Gpa got to the sidewalk, the Raconteur called out to him. "Charlie, everybody respects the road trip, man." He held his hand in the air to Gpa and flashed him peace.

Gpa let out a little sniff of a laugh and smiled. "Keep on trucking, Lou," he said, and they nodded to each other with miles in their eyes.

Then Gpa turned back around and we all piled into the Blue Bomber.

Corrina was the only one who'd changed clothes. I was in my usual blue jeans and T-shirt, and Gpa was still half hidden beneath his veterans' cap, and Corrina had gotten back into her black jeans, but with a different T-shirt, one with the sleeves ripped off and rolled into a tank top. Some band I'd never heard of was silkscreened in black and white on the front. They all looked skinny and close to death.

Corrina got the car rolling out of the Raconteur's neighborhood, put the skyline of the Strip behind us, and the dusty RV parks and faded fast-food joints and Big Lots and other discount stores all ticked by along the flat, colorless highway like the slow blades of an enormous fan.

We fought through traffic on the backside of Paradise, but once we passed the last cluster of cookie-cutter, prefab, white-box homes in Henderson, we were back out on the open road with the pale blue sky an infinite expanse all around us. We could have been on the moon and I wouldn't have cared, because I was with everyone I wanted to be with. I glanced at Corrina—who was hidden behind her round, gold-rimmed sunglasses, and who sang along with the pulsing power chord song on her playlist—and smiled at her.

We put miles of highway behind us and wound our way toward the Hoover Dam as Corrina kept the Blue Bomber heading east to Arizona. We found ourselves on a bridge with a few hills in front of us and the vast gray sweep of desert beyond, but then the road dipped down and down and kept winding down, and what I thought were hills were the rocks piled highest on the gigantic mounds of earth that became steep cliff faces of the largest gorge I had ever seen, and the reddish-gray rock of Nevada was behind us and the reddish-maroon rock of Arizona was ahead of us and the green snake of the Colorado River divided it all, far below. High above, the clouds stretched like flamboyant quills.

We were on our way. Gpa was quiet and calm and mostly staring out the window, listening to contemporary musicians Corrina kept steady-flowing through the speakers, and for a stony, butte-strewn, mountainous stretch of miles, a strange peace came over me, a sense that this ridiculous plan might actually come together after all, just like the seamlessness of miles and miles of music from Corrina's own playlist: Sarah Jaffe, Hindi Zahra, the Heavy, Pimps of Joytime, Gary Clark, Jr., Little Hurricane, We Are Trees, the Districts.

But somewhere just after we merged onto the 40 near Kingman and passed the surreal green golf courses surrounded by the desert brown, beige, and gray, Corrina's phone started buzzing and rattling in the dashboard dock. We both glanced at the image of her father's pinched and ruddy face staring at us from the screen. He looked so much older than I thought he was, balding, some thin, feathery hair still clinging to his head, eyes that looked yellow with exhaustion. In the photo, he wasn't wearing glasses, but they'd left red indents on the bridge of his nose.

Corrina ignored the call. "Go away," she said to the phone.

He rang again, and a third time, and Corrina growled in frustration. "Just make him go away," she said. Thinking

I was being helpful, I reached for the phone and was going to hit the switch to flick off the screen, but the car lurched and my hand swayed and my finger stabbed the answer button.

The buzzing stopped, the music paused, and Corrina's father's tinny voice tore into the car. "Corrina? Corrina? Where are you?" It wasn't on speakerphone, so he sounded mousy and distant, but he repeated himself and pleaded with her to respond.

Corrina whacked the steering wheel and turned to look at me. I couldn't see her eyes behind her sunglasses, but I knew she was glaring at me. I was too embarrassed to move, too scared to say anything. I sat rigid and quiet as if the seat belt had tied my arms back and roped itself around my mouth. The Blue Bomber picked up speed.

"Corrina, please," her father continued. "Where are you? What are you doing?"

"Well, answer him," Gpa said from the backseat. He leaned forward and pointed at the phone. "Is that your father? Talk to the man."

"Corrina?"

But before Gpa or her father could say anything else, Corrina hung up. Her father's face disappeared and she didn't look at me. "Hendrix, you idiot," she said to the road ahead of us.

"I'm sorry. It was an accident."

We ripped at a speed that made the car feel like it was

rocking on the wheels, and I was about to ask her to slow down, but she floored it, cut off a car in the middle lane when she swooped in front of it, and then swerved across the exit lane and steered onto the wide rocky lip along the side of the highway, braking in the gravel, skidding, and almost losing control.

"Hey!" Gpa yelled.

"What the hell?" I said.

As soon as she put the Blue Bomber in park and shut off the engine, she jumped out of the driver's side and scurried up the slope. I followed her at first, leaving the door open, and Old Humper bolted out behind me into the wasteland of sagebrush beside the highway. I was suddenly terrified he'd come tearing back and run out onto the highway, but I heard Gpa's door open too. I turned to him. He stood close to the car, but on the side with the traffic rushing past him at ninety miles an hour. He stretched his arms. I ran back to him.

"Come on, Gpa," I said when I was beside him. "Let's go get Old Humper."

"Don't call him that. His name's Skipper." Gpa was grumpy, but he let me guide him around the trunk to the lip and up the slope. I could see Old Humper in the near distance by a large rock. Corrina stood with her hands on her hips. "That girl is crazy," he said as we approached her.

She kept her back to us. "Damnit," she said.

"Hey," I said. "You can't just do that."

"Don't tell me what to do."

"You could have killed us. What if the car had spun out? What if another car had been too close? I'm serious, Corrina. That was stupid."

She turned to me. "I already have one dad, Hendrix. I don't need another."

"What are you, nuts?" Frankly, I was freaked out. I couldn't even keep my hands still—I had to thrust them in my pockets just to keep them from shaking. Why wasn't she scared? She just stood there, staring me down, like we were two dogs about to dive at each other. Was she *ever* scared? Truthfully, I didn't even believe that tough-girl act. She probably didn't realize what she'd done—but that kind of obliviousness and recklessness was as spooky as Gpa's delusions or black holes of thought.

"I'm sorry, all right?" I said. "But did you even see him get out of the car? On the side with traffic?" I pointed to Gpa, trying to be subtle, but he noticed anyway.

"I'm right here, Teddy. I'm not invisible."

"Jesus, seriously," Corrina said. "Stop worrying so goddamn much. It's annoying."

"I'm not the problem here. That was dangerous!"

"Stop shouting at me," Corrina said.

"Look," I said, quieting. "I'm sorry I answered the phone. It was an accident."

"Sorry, sorry, sorry." Corrina glanced at her phone again, then put it in her back pocket and marched into the sage desert, but in a different direction than Old Humper.

"Well," Gpa said as we watched her walk away. "You should probably go after her."

"I don't think so," I said.

"Listen," Gpa said. "You can't let someone walk away like that. A person usually wants—"

"Gpa, you don't have all the answers all the time," I said. Then I took a breath. "Please. Just let her be."

Gpa frowned and called after Old Humper.

It wasn't that I didn't want to chase after Corrina—I did—but in the last few days I'd heard her ask for silence, I'd watched her take her space. The least I could do was respect that, especially after I had answered the damn phone like an idiot, bringing her father into the car, wrecking that whole sense of freedom we'd had so far. I'm sure he didn't know who I was, or Gpa, or that Corrina could be with us, but I was worried what he might do, that somehow, on only this second day on the road, he could do something to stop us, to reel us back in before we'd even gotten that far. That was what fathers did, didn't they? Show their power, both when you wanted it and when you didn't?

Of course, I didn't really know.

Much farther down the road, clouds gathered and cast a shadow over the desert. I watched Corrina walk a small circle and stop and stare ahead at the same clouds. To my right, Gpa had found something like a stick, and he played fetch with Old Humper.

"Hey," I said to him. "Last night. We didn't get to talk."

"That's all we did was talk," Gpa said.

"I mean about my dad," I said.

He remained quiet.

"Gpa, he's my dad. Shouldn't I know him more?"

"It was years ago, Teddy."

"But what happened? Why won't you and Mom talk about him?"

"You heard. He was having an affair." Gpa picked up the stick again and whipped it ahead with more force. "Right there, under my own damn nose, all the way back home in Ithaca. And I thought he was coming to see his sick mother on all those trips." He looked back at me. "That's what your mother thought too, you know." Old Humper brought him the stick and Gpa wrestled with him to pull it out of his mouth. Gpa was the only one who played rough with Old Humper—they both liked it. "There's not a lot more to say."

"But come on. I mean, am I like him at all?"

Gpa let go of the stick and turned back to me. "No, Teddy." He walked to me and put his hand on my shoulder. "You're nothing like him."

"You can't just make him disappear. Why would you want to?"

"Teddy," Gpa grumbled. "You can't possibly understand. Your mother and I just thought it best not to bring him up. There was no point in making you miss him more."

Old Humper bounced in between us and looked up at

Gpa. Stick still in his mouth, joyfully shaking his butt.

"And besides," Gpa continued, "you have no idea how angry he made me. What he did to your mother. What he did to me and your grandmother. I never forgave him, Teddy."

He bent down to Old Humper and pulled the stick away quickly.

"But—" I said.

"No," Gpa said, turning away from me and throwing the stick. "This interview is over."

He walked a few paces away, following Old Humper, and I let him go. Corrina was still about thirty yards ahead, staring down at her phone, then looking up at the darkening horizon. She put one hand to her head and held it there, and I was too far away to see the expression on her face, but for some reason, it reminded me of my mom, an image I had of her before she was corporate Mom, the boxy gray suit, the stone-stiff statue without emotion, way back from around the time my dad died, and I didn't know if it had been before or after, but the image was as clear as if I was staring at a photograph.

Mom sat on the living room couch, surrounded by piles of recently washed laundry she was about to fold, and, having found a pair of Dead Dad's underwear, she had begun to cry. She put it on her head, wore it like a mask, and sobbed loudly, moaning, half hidden beneath her terrifying costume.

Maybe Mom needed the suit to keep her from falling apart again?

Gpa was busy with Old Humper, so I walked over to

Corrina. It smelled like rain, as if, even though I stepped through the dust, I could taste water in the air around me.

"Hey," I said to her.

"Hey."

"Let me ask you this," I said. "Do you want to turn around and head back?"

"No," she said. "We just got started. Besides, they wouldn't even know I was gone if I hadn't lifted the thousand dollars from the cash drawer in my dad's office." She beamed a fake smile.

"Oh, shit."

"Don't look at me like that. We stole your mom's car. I had to steal something too. Plus, how the hell was I going to pay for anything when we split up?"

She looked at me for a long moment. "And where exactly am I going, anyway, Hendrix? What am I doing? You have somewhere to go. Ithaca. Where am I going?"

"I don't know. Maybe there's something in Ithaca for you, too."

"I doubt it." She kicked at the dirt. "I want a shot at something big. I don't want to just be the girl who hung around some parties. I want a shot to play for someone important. I want a real shot, Hendrix."

"I agree."

She looked up suddenly. "Aiko!" she shouted. "Aiko! Oh my God, the Electric Warts are so big now and they're in Brooklyn. I have to call her."

When we got to Gpa, Old Humper was in strict obey mode, heeling by Gpa's feet, and Gpa himself seemed to be in command mode, one hand clasping the other behind his back, shoulders square. He tipped his head toward the east. The clouds had already smothered the mountains ahead, and more spilled out over the desert like gigantic gray waves rising just before they break. "It's coming quickly," he said. "Teddy. Let's get that, you know, Blue Bomber, on the move. Rain'll be here any minute." His expression was still and those brilliant blue eyes clear and present, and for a moment I had a flash of the old Gpa, the one I'd known just a few years earlier, the one who could hide a subtle smirk inside an order, as if he was laughing at himself behind a straight face.

"How you doing, Gpa?"

"This ain't paradise," he said, and winked. "Now, let's get going."

And down we went, Old Humper staying closer to Gpa after only one look and one word (*Heel!*), all of us clambering back into the Blue Bomber, Gpa checking the seat belt around Corrina's guitar, the windows going up, Corrina starting the car.

"To Ithaca," she said.

"To Brooklyn," I said.

"Oh, yeah," she said. "There's a song for that." She fiddled with the phone until she found it. "Beastie Boys. *Licensed to Ill*. 1986. 'No Sleep Till Brooklyn.'"

And it played as the Blue Bomber kicked up gravel and we

pulled out into the right lane and then picked up speed and crossed two lanes to the left, and around us the whole desert sank into a deeper shade of gray as the rain came down and washed the dust from the rocks and the brush and cast us all into a dark, midday kind of night.

CHAPTER 13

DESERT STORMS

There were two things I had not considered before we left: how often we would need to get gas, and where we were going to sleep each night.

Corrina pointed to a sign as we blew past it. "What'd that say?"

"'Grand Canyon sixty-two miles.'"

Then we passed a sign that indicated the next two exits were for the Grand Canyon—sixty miles to the north.

"What I'm looking for," Corrina said, "is a sign for gas. We're hovering too close to empty."

"Great," I said. "We'll stop at the next station."

"Hendrix?"

"Yeah?" I was still floating from my moment inspiring Corrina, and despite the rain, enjoying the ride up into the high-desert forests.

"Have you seen a gas station anytime recently?"

"No."

"This is serious."

I looked back at Gpa, who was asleep, and then thought about what would happen if the car ran out of gas and we drifted to a stop at the side of the road in Arizona and how we'd be stuck without phone reception, and as soon as someone did help us, they'd have to find out who we were and we'd be shipped back to LA, failures.

We were quiet for a few more miles, until we finally saw a sign for a Mobil. It was along the highway, but when we pulled into it, there was a man in coveralls pulling plastic trash bags over the pumps. "No good," he told us. "I'm out of gas."

"How is that even possible?" I asked as we got back on the road.

"Hendrix, we are in the middle of nowhere," Corrina said.

We got back onto the 40 and kept heading toward Flagstaff. Corrina didn't sing along with the music.

Twenty miles down the road we saw another sign for gas. The station was just off the highway, only a hundred yards off the exit on the access road. It was called Feed and Mercantile, with the Texaco pumps out front, and the station had a short green roof hovering over a front porch, complete with a little wooden railing I imagined one might tie a horse to if one had one, and if anybody still did that kind of thing.

Two old men sat slumped up next to each other like dried apricots on a wooden bench that looked like it might collapse if anyone else joined them. They smoked and remained motionless as they watched us pull in. We parked in front of a pump and I jumped out to figure out how to fill the tank. Corrina had filled it the day before. I lifted the nozzle and the switch and followed the directions, but no gas came out. I was under the black-and-red Texaco awning, but the rain swept in sideways and beaded against my face. I looked around the pump and the apricots stared at me. The pump in front of us had a piece of paper partially taped to it, so I jogged to it and tried to read it, but it was ripped in half and the blue ink was smeared, making it illegible.

Corrina opened her door. "You have to pay cash up front sometimes," she said over the rain's attack against the plastic and metal awning.

But that wasn't it, and I knew it. I climbed back into the car, before I got any more soaked.

"They don't have gas here, either?" Corrina asked. "Jesus, the whole area must be out."

"What do we do?" I asked.

"Let's see if we can make it to Flagstaff."

But when she turned the key in the ignition, nothing happened. There was a revving in the engine, but nothing turned on. "Shit," Corrina said. She hit the wheel. "I should have kept the motor running." She tried the key again and again but nothing happened.

"We're out of gas," Gpa said from the backseat. "You'll fry the transmission if you keep turning that key." I hadn't realized he had woken up, but now that he was awake, I was glad he was with us, and really with us.

"What do we do?" I asked him.

"Find gas," he said. "That's it."

Corrina put her head down on the wheel. "I can't believe I let it get this low," she said. "Before they got the electric, the ex-hippies had a rule about gas in the car. Never let it drop beneath a quarter tank. The one time I ignore that. The one time!" She lifted her head and stared out into the rain.

I pulled out my phone, but we were in a dead zone.

"We can't just sit here," Gpa said.

"I know," I said, but I saw he was about to step out of the car. "No," I said. "I'll ask inside."

The rain picked up and whipped me as I ran over to the porch. I stomped my wet feet by the front door and glanced at the apricots. Up close, I could see they both had thick white mustaches, and they both blinked and squinted, but said nothing.

"Can we get any gas here?" I asked them.

They rolled their gummy lips but said nothing. They turned their heads back to the car, or the distance, or whatever the hell was running through their minds, and I went inside.

The convenience store was packed with Route 66 memorabilia and T-shirts and candy on the shelves and beer and soda in the two narrow refrigerators. Two ceiling fans spun slowly overhead. The cash register and lotto station were on a small desk built from the same slats of wood that covered the walls of the store. The lights were dim and warm, and maybe because of the rain, the store seemed cozy and inviting. Nobody else was in the store, but I heard the faint sounds of music coming from another room, and through a narrow wooden doorway I could see large plastic bags stacked on shelves, and I walked around the desk to that room. The bags tuned out to be sacks of grain and pellets for horses and poultry, and again, no one else was in the room, but the music was a little louder, or I could just hear it better, I wasn't sure, nor was I really sure if it was music, or if it was just voices that sounded musical, but they were so damn interesting, because they pulled me toward them even though they seemed to be coming through the walls.

The rest of the store was still empty, and because the music was traveling through me now like an itch I couldn't scratch away, I walked around to the front and to the hallway where I'd seen the sign for the restroom and found another little hallway with a row of post office boxes and a door half ajar at the far end. The sound was coming from behind the door, and now it was clearer to me that it was voices, but in a language I couldn't understand, or one that seemed familiar but like in a distant, barely recognizable memory. Through the open door, I could see bales of hay along the cement-block wall, straw spread across the floor, and the skinned pelts of small animals hanging from the ceiling.

When I emerged into the small, makeshift barn, I saw two white girls about my age or a little older standing near the back wall, swaying and looking down near their feet, droning with a kind of undulating, melodic wail. I was immediately embarrassed that I'd walked in on them, but also mesmerized by what appeared to be a funeral they were holding for what looked like a dog in a hole they'd dug in the ground by their feet.

They didn't turn to face me, or even seem to know I was there, and I would have dumbly stood there in the doorway to the barn forever if Corrina hadn't suddenly grabbed my shoulder and pulled me back into the hallway with the post office boxes. The wailing sang on behind us, unbroken, like the thump and the hiss of the surf on a cold, dark night back in Venice.

"What are you doing?" Corrina asked as she dragged me out to the front of the store.

"I don't know," I said. "I heard it and I had to find out what it was."

"You look like you were in a dream."

"They were holding a funeral."

"That's depressing," Corrina said. "And creepy. This whole place is creepy."

"And no gas," I said.

She led me out onto the front porch past the apricots and back out into the rain. She pointed around the other side of station. "There's a little driveway," she said. "I can see something else down there. Cars. A garage. Let's go check it out."

She started to walk away, but I grabbed her arm. "We can't just leave Gpa on his own back here," I said. "What if he wanders?"

"What? He'd do that?"

"He could," I said.

Corrina nodded toward the garage. "Look," she said. "The driveway to the next garage runs downhill. Maybe we can push the car down there."

We doubled back to the Blue Bomber and Corrina explained what we needed to do. I didn't have a clue about how we could possibly manage pushing a car, but once she got it in neutral and we pushed it out from under the awning, we realized we could do it. Gpa wanted to help, too. The window was down, and he shouted from the backseat.

"Let me out," he said. "I'll help push."

"No," I said.

"Don't tell me what I can and can't do, Teddy," he said.

We were pushing slowly and not getting very far, and we could have used help, but what if he slipped and hit his head? What if he fell and the car rolled over him?

Corrina yelled over the hood of the car to me.

"Hendrix," she said. "We need a driver. Someone has to steer." She was right. We were pointed in a straight line toward a stand of trees. We had to get the car curving to the left to get it into the driveway. We squinted through the heavy rain and held our hands over our eyes like visors, and Corrina smiled at me. "We need a captain!" she shouted so Gpa could hear her through the window. "We need your help, man. Get behind the wheel."

She looked at me again. "We can do it!" I wanted to freeze time, slide across the hood, wrap her in my arms, and tell her the secret in my heart that I now knew was absolutely true, because when you see the most beautiful girl in the world with rain plastering her hair to her head, her T-shirt slick and stuck to her like a second skin, and she reads the signs and cares for your Gpa even better than you, that secret you've tried not to admit to yourself ignites and spreads through your body like the sun breaking through night into day.

We got Gpa up in the driver's seat, and with his help we got the Blue Bomber carving an arc in the mud toward the driveway. "Hell yeah!" Corrina yelled, and I yelled too, just something guttural and animal and free like I hadn't felt before, and the car even started picking up a little speed and got easier to roll, until suddenly we realized the hill was steeper than we'd thought and the car was rolling free on its own without us pushing it and instead of pushing at the front of the open windows we switched to the back of the windows and tried to hold it back but the car was too heavy and began to accelerate down the short hill. We had to jog to keep up with it.

"Brake!" Corrina yelled. "Brake!"

"Brake!" I echoed.

Gpa had two hands on the wheel and was at least keeping a straight line, but now it seemed like the Blue Bomber might go slamming into the metal door of the garage down the hill. It gained more speed and we started to run alongside it.

"Charlie!" Corrina yelled. "Brake, goddamnit!"

"I am," he said. And he was. The wheels had stopped spinning. They just slid down the hill in the ruts they'd formed in the red mud. The Blue Bomber kept its course for the door, and I thought Gpa was actually going to ram it, but he turned the wheel and the tires broke through the rut, the car angled and slowed, and as we got to the bottom of the slope, onto flat ground, the car came to a stop a few feet away from the garage.

Our hearts raced, mud caked our legs, but we were safe.

"Roll up the windows, Charlie," Corrina said. "We'll be right back."

"Don't go anywhere," I added, but he frowned and shook his head at me.

There was a glass door in the side shop next to the garage, and as Corrina and I walked to it, I could see a few people inside. We opened the door and stepped inside, and three men, each of them the size of two men, stopped what they were doing and looked at us.

Actually, it almost seemed like there were six heads in the room, the three bald heads of the supersized men, and the skulls with fire coming out of their eyes and mouths on their

T-shirts. One stood behind the makeshift counter, which looked like a section of an old fence. Another sat in a chair tilted onto the back two legs, resting his motorcycle boots on the counter. And the third sat on a stool across from him, but he stood when we entered. The skull stretched out over his chest looked bigger than my head.

The one behind the counter was whistling, but as we came in, the man in the chair hollered. "Damnit, none of us know what song that is, but you got it stuck in my head. Just quit it already, unless you can tell me what the hell it is you think you're whistling!"

The man behind the counter shrugged. "I don't know."

The man on the stool, the largest of the three, glared at us. "Looking for something?" he asked.

"Gas," Corrina said.

"Pumps out front," he said slowly.

"Are empty," Corrina finished for him.

He looked her up and down as slowly as he spoke. They all stared at Corrina, at her T-shirt, at the band, I guess, or maybe they all were just ogling her. They didn't seem to give a shit if they scared us. In fact, they were enjoying it.

"Long way from home, little man," the one behind the counter said to me.

They all had long beards, but the beards made them look older than I thought they probably were. They could have been brothers. I thought of the girls back up by the shop. But the garage was a kind of shop too. There were a few stands of shelves with a slim selection of windshield wiper fluid, anti-freeze, and oil; wiper blades, rags, and rubber mats; and yes, red plastic gallon containers of gas.

"Where you from?" the guy standing asked Corrina.

"LA," she said.

I pointed to the gas on the shelf. "How much is the gas?" I asked.

The first man took a step closer. "LA?" he said to Corrina. "You are a long way from home." He looked at me. "You like a little south of the border?"

He grinned, and he was as ugly as the skull on his shirt. The guy behind the counter laughed, but the guy in the chair swung his legs down, slamming the chair legs to the ground. The *pop* on the floor made me jump.

"We watched you coming down here," he said. "Someone else with you?"

"My grandfather," I said.

He shook his head. "Where you going?"

"New York."

That made him laugh, and the others followed him. "Whole lot of country between LA and New York."

"How much for the gas?" Corrina said. She walked over to the shelf and grabbed two of the gallon containers.

"How much they worth to you?" the guy in the chair asked Corrina. He leaned forward and put his hands between his knees.

"How much is the gas?" I asked. I was trembling like crazy

on the inside and hoped I didn't show it on the outside. "We're in a hurry," I added.

"Of course you are," the guy in the chair said. "How much you willing to pay for it?"

I put my hand in my pocket, about to fish out my wallet like a major frigging idiot, when the door opened behind me. The rain swept in and Gpa put his hand on my shoulder. He steered around me and walked to Corrina. "Find the gas?" he asked. I thought maybe he didn't notice, but then, as he put his hand on her back and stared at the three beards, I realized Gpa had understood the situation as soon as he'd entered.

"They found it," the guy in the chair said. He looked at Gpa and saw the cap on his head. His expression changed. "You a marine?"

"'Sixty-seven to 'sixty-nine. Khe Sanh. Hue," Gpa said. "You?"

"Fallujah."

Gpa nodded, walked across the room, and shook his hand. The other guys relaxed. The big one who'd been on the stool went around the counter. "Hey," the vet said. "Ring these kids up."

Corrina and I brought four gallons of gas to the counter and Corrina added two bottles of dry gas, and as we paid for them and bagged them with the guys behind the counter, Gpa spoke in halting, almost coded, phrases and fragments of sentences about urban warfare, Fallujah and Baghdad, and Hue in Vietnam.

The vet even followed us outside and helped us get the

gas in the car and made sure we could start it up. Once we did, Gpa shook hands with him again and said something low in his ear. The man nodded. "Sorry for the trouble," he said. "No disrespect. Just having a little fun."

Gpa nodded. "Thanks for the help."

Corrina stuck her head out the window and raised her gaze over the stretched skull, up to the vet's eyes. "Ted Nugent," she said to him.

"What?"

"Ted Nugent. 'Call of the Wild.' 1974. He can't whistle for shit, but that's the song. Song sucks, too, by the way."

She started the engine, angled the Blue Bomber back away from the station, and left the vet standing by himself in the mud as she got us back up the hill. "Those guys were assholes," she said as she pulled out onto the access road in front of the Feed and Mercantile. "Assholes."

"Look," Gpa said. "He needed to see the situation in a different light."

"Bros. Brahs. Old boys' club. Same damn shit," Corrina continued.

"Well, most people respect the road trip," Gpa said. "I mean, when you get down to it, everyone respects the road trip."

CHAPTER 14

GRAY HALLUCINATIONS

Corrina got the Blue Bomber back out onto the 40 and pushed us ahead toward Flagstaff. I watched the storm attack the peak of Mount Humphreys ahead. Lightning flashed again and again, as if some horrific battle was taking place in the sky.

One thing all three of us agreed. The assholes had made us hungry. Eventually we saw signs for Flagstaff, and as we approached the city I hoped we'd find something. First we topped up the gas tank, then we found a taco joint and sat in a booth trying not to look like outlaws on the run. Gpa was quiet, and although he'd been alert and energetic at the garage, he napped again shortly after we got back on the highway, and I worried his mind was tired. When the waiter asked him what he wanted, he paused. He took a deep breath, and I saw the confusion rising in his face.

"Hey, Gpa," I said. "Let's get what we always get. You like the chicken burrito and I like the carnitas. We should just get those, right?"

He glanced up at me and smiled. "Yes," he said. "Of course."

The restaurant had a vaulted ceiling, colorful booths raised up on a platform along one wall, tables scattered beside that, and a long bar, behind which an enormous plastic shark busted through the fake bricks. Other nautically related items hung on the walls or from the ceiling, surfboards, lobster traps, scuba diving signs indicating "wet spots" with not so subtle other undertones, foam buoys and other plastic fish. I liked the feel of the place, but the bar music was loud and echoing in the cavernous space, four large-screen TVs flashed at different points throughout the restaurant, and the din of customers and the wait staff all added up to a very non-Gpa-friendly choice.

We got our food, and soon after, Gpa had to go to the bathroom. I led the way and waited in the restroom while he managed and cleaned up, and when we walked back into the restaurant, he held me tightly by the arm. I got him back in the booth, but he looked down at his plate as if he'd already forgotten what it was, and when he looked around, his eyes moved quickly, as if he'd just woken from a nap and he didn't remember having fallen asleep.

"Where the hell are we, again?" he asked.

"Flagstaff," Corrina said.

He nodded, but I could tell he was struggling to place her.

"We're on a road trip," I said to him. "We're having a blast."

Corrina picked up on Gpa's struggle immediately.

"Everybody respects the road trip, Charlie," she said, using his own line.

He scowled and went back to eating. We all ate in silence for a few moments, but Corrina was looking around at the place skeptically too. In addition to the nautical theme, there were sombreros everywhere. Not hanging on the wall by themselves, but perched on the heads of sharks, or on the heads of grossly cartooned men depicted in signs and posters on the walls. I'd walked into the place and not even noticed at first: Every single person in the restaurant was white, except Corrina.

"I picked a stupid place for lunch," I said. "I'm noticing that now."

"You think?" she said, taking another forkful of her enchilada. "Food's not bad, but give me a fucking break."

"I know," I said.

"What's with the mouth?" Gpa said from across the table. He glared at Corrina. "If I'm taking you out to lunch, I'd like a little decorum here."

"Uh, okay," Corrina said. She looked at me.

"You too," Gpa said to me. "You just expect me to take you out every time we see each other and you have no respect for the way I raised you."

He waved his fork at me as he spoke, and Corrina stared at me. I wasn't sure what was going on. I always paid for burritos back at Holy Guacamole by the beach, or rather, I had money from Mom, and I was also paying for everything on the road.

"I don't have to make these trips," Gpa went on. "I come down here to see you and this is always the case. Another lunch, another girl. We eat. We go. How about you ask how your mother is doing?"

"Gpa?" I said.

"Jake, you have no idea what we did so you could have the life we've given you. No idea! How about a little respect?"

Anger boiled in his pinched eyes, and I wasn't sure how to get him to calm down. Although my back was to most of the restaurant, I was sure some people could hear us. The ghost was back, sitting at lunch with us, but this time he was in me.

"Gpa," I whispered. "It's me, Teddy."

He breathed through his nose. "What is going on here?" he said.

"Do me a favor," Corrina said. "Let's sing that early Joni Mitchell song, that one you told me you and Betty loved."

Corrina sang a few lines and then reached for his hand, but he batted it away, knocking her hand into the wall beside her. "Cut that out," he said. "Don't tease me. Oh, Jake," he said, shaking his head at me. "You and your girls. You and all your girls." He sniffed bitterly. "Who is this, again? Who am I supposed to get to know today?"

"Gpa, hey," I said, louder this time, not giving a damn if others could hear us now. I put my arm around Corrina. "It's me, Teddy. We're just getting burritos, like we always do. This is my friend, Corrina. She's driving us. I love you. I'm doing everything you asked. I always do. Let's just enjoy our burritos, okay?"

I spoke as calmly and evenly as I could, and then, without thinking, I took Corrina's hand in mine. She let me take it, and when I squeezed, she squeezed back, and somehow I didn't have to even look at her and I knew she wasn't mad.

"I don't understand," Gpa said.

"Gpa," I said. "I'd like to take you back to the car."

"I don't understand," he said again, and I watched the cloudy-eyed confusion of one of his bad days drift over him. This was worse than when he simply lost words, like *refrigerator* or *soup*; it was much scarier, as if he was living in another time, as if he was looking at the world in double exposure, a gray hallucination of the past imprinted on the one we were living in now.

I stood and gave Corrina a wad of cash and she simply nodded, and I came around the other side of the booth and tried to help Gpa out of his seat. He struggled a little at first, but his fury had subsided, and in his confusion, he was more afraid than angry. I got him out to the car and into the backseat with Old Humper; the seat was a little wet, because we'd had to keep the windows open for Old Humper, but it had stopped raining and the air was cool and crisp and the giant cumulus clouds drifted slowly by like ships in the enormous harbor of the sky, and I looked up into it as I leaned against the Blue Bomber and read from the HFB, telling Gpa a story he'd once told me.

THE STORY OF GPA AND GMA'S FIRST KISS

Betty McCarthy was the absolute beauty of Ithaca. Her parents thought this beauty would be her ticket to happiness. They also thought happiness was wealth and security. Her parents were wrong.

In 1963 there weren't many wealthy people in Ithaca who weren't in some way connected to Cornell or Ithaca College. But some kids who weren't professors' kids still looked like they had some promise. Charlie Hendrix was not one of those kids, but his friend Frank Morris was. Everybody knew Frank was going to be a doctor or a lawyer or a senator. His old man managed a garage on the edge of town. He hadn't made it through high school, but Frank had been valedictorian, and he had plans of going places. Everybody knew that. Everybody expected it. And everybody in town knew Frank. Frank got free floats at Purity Ice Cream when he took a date there. The bartender at Macavoy's always gave Frank's date a free sherry when they arrived. Everybody knew Frank, and everybody loved Frank, especially Frank. He and Gpa worked together at Frank's father's garage, and this supposedly made them friends, but they didn't hang out much.

On the night Frank was supposed to take Betty

to Macavoy's for their first date, he'd forgotten that he'd already made plans with Kim Lynch, whom he'd been seeing in private, and with whom he'd had plans of his own.

"Take Betty for me, will you, Charlie? Let Davy know on the sly you're doing me a favor. He'll set you up."

"It's a date. You can't just swap the man."

"Ha! No, you can't, can you. But do a friend a favor."

Charlie reluctantly agreed, and when he showed up at Betty's door, she thought it was a joke. She made him sit there, on the front steps of her porch, so they could wait for Frank and she could tell him how rude he was, and how she'd always known he'd had mean blood running through him. Charlie tried to console her, tried to tell her Frank was all right, but he wasn't convincing because he, himself, was not at all convinced that was true, and after a while he told her the truth about Frank. Well, most of it. He didn't say a word about Kim, because who was he to say a bad thing about her.

"Well, that settles it," Betty said. "I didn't get dressed up for nothing." She looked at Charlie's car. "Charlie Hendrix," she said. "You are not going to be a doctor, or a professor, and truth is you are a little shorter than any man I'd let take me on a date, but you've been sitting here with me on my parents' porch for an hour and you haven't complained once."

"Well, I like your company."

Betty rolled her eyes.

"I do. But mostly, it's for your voice."

At this she laughed. Most boys said other stupid things about her when they complimented her. None had ever said anything stupid about her voice. None until Charlie.

"You're angry, but you don't sound it. All I hear is something earnest. You're not mad at Frank as much as you're shocked that indecency like his even exists in the world."

"I am," she said. "It's so much easier to be honest."

"I agree."

She smiled. "Are you planning to take me to Macavoy's?"

"Truth is, Betty, I'd rather not take you there. Just doesn't seem the right place. And even though I know there's a free sherry waiting for you there, I'd rather go somewhere else, even if I have to stretch for it."

"Do you have a blanket in your car?"

"I do."

"Then I have an idea."

This worried Gpa immediately.

"I'll say this," Gma then continued. "At least you have a car, Charlie."

She directed him through town, northeast, into the hills, and on the way she asked if Gpa was a gentleman and Gpa said he was. "How can I know?" Gma asked.

"What would it take to prove it?"

"You won't try to kiss me tonight."

"I won't."

She directed him to a field, a clearing on a hillside, a slope like a natural amphitheater looking out over Lake Cayuga and the infinity of night. They watched the stars swim slowly through the sky. They talked about their lives growing up. They were three years apart, they'd gone to the same high school, and Gpa was shocked she'd remembered him when he was a senior. She was finishing college now, at Ithaca. He'd been working at the Morrises' garage, saving everything he could, and planned to open his own garage soon. They made each other laugh. What they both knew without saying it was that they trusted each other. And finally, when it had gotten late, and Gpa would have to take Gma home soon, she told him it was okay.

"You can kiss me."

"No," Gpa said.

She laughed. "No. It's okay. I don't mind."

"No. I'd be breaking my promise," he said. "And that's no way to start something I want to continue. I keep my promises."

"Oh!" She whacked him on the shoulder. "Don't be stubborn. You'll ruin the moment."

"No," he said again. "But I will ask a favor."

"The nerve!"

"Would you let me bring you back here tomorrow night?"

They went back to the same spot the next night, and with their hearts pounding and getting in the way of what had been easier conversation the night before, Gma couldn't wait any longer, and she beat Gpa to his line.

"Good God, Charlie, can I please kiss you and get this over with?"

"Yes," he said, and she did.

After a while they paused, and they were silent for a moment.

"Now," Gpa said, taking Gma's hand. "Can I kiss you again?"

She laughed and the night was perfect, with only one exception—Gpa felt a little guilty that he got her home a half hour late.

I read it all to him through the open window while we waited for Corrina to pay the bill, and by the time I finished, he was nodding and remembering along with me.

"Teddy?" he asked, and I was glad he was back with me again. I opened the door and he stepped out and leaned against the Blue Bomber beside me. "This is awful."

"I know."

We'd only been on the road one day and I was already beginning to wonder if I'd made the right choice. I just wanted to keep my promise, and I didn't want doing that to hurt him more.

CHAPTER 15

CAMPFIRE

Eventually Corrina came out and we put the leash on Old Humper and took him around the neighborhood for a walk to stretch his legs and let him go buck-wild if he needed to, because I thought I understood what it was to feel a little crazy and act a little crazy and feel the need to shake that craziness out once in a while and not keep it bottled up inside you like a bomb waiting to go off in some sudden, unexplainable moment in the future.

Gpa held the leash, since Old Humper listened to him better than me or Corrina, and we walked downhill toward the edge of the neighborhood, to look out over another part of Flagstaff that dipped below.

"Sorry about all that," I said to Corrina as we walked behind Gpa and Old Humper.

"No, don't worry," she said. "I'm getting used to it. You just have to go with it. You give a little and play in his world, and that's cool, and then you slowly walk him back into ours."

"How's your hand?" I asked.

"It's fine. But shit is fucked up, Hendrix. The sign? The logo? Sombrero-wearing shark, and the shark has a big thick black mustache? And the dude behind the bar, a white dude, was wearing the same sombrero and had a fake mustache too." She swatted at the air in front of her. "That's what scares me. That guy plays racist Halloween every day of his life?" She glanced up at me. "Seriously, Hendrix, I don't know if the asshole at the garage or the clueless dude behind the bar is worse. That's what scares me. Not your Gpa."

"Well, sorry about that."

"Stop apologizing, Hendrix. That doesn't fix anything. Think about where we're going to sleep tonight."

"Oh, yeah," I said. "I hadn't thought about that."

"Yeah," Corrina said. "Exactly."

We were both quiet a moment. My brain felt like it could explode. I had to think about Gpa, but I also couldn't stop thinking about what Corrina had just said. It was so weird. It was like my whiteness just put pirate patches over my eyes and I was blind to all the pain. I wasn't the guys in the garage or the guys at the restaurant, but if I didn't try a lot harder to take the damn blinders off and say what I saw, then I sure as hell was more like those guys than I wanted to be.

Corrina was right. And she was right that we had to find a place to sleep.

"Look," I said. "I don't know if we should drive on today. I mean, we could. We probably should. But it might be better just to keep it low-key with Gpa."

When we'd made the new route at the Raconteur's we'd planned to stay in Albuquerque our first night out of Vegas—an eight-hour drive or so, without traffic. From there, the next day, a nine-hour drive to somewhere outside of Oklahoma City. But we were only in Flagstaff and I'd pushed Gpa enough that day. I resolved to do more takeout, if we could, for the rest of the drive.

It was already evening by the time we found our accommodations. The place was on a hill just outside of Flagstaff and it looked more like a log cabin amid the woods than a motel or B&B, but the rain and heavy clouds had swept away and there were what sounded like a thousand tiny birds chirping in the pine trees around the cabin. We were all glad to be out of the car for the rest of the day, especially Old Humper, who spun a few circles and tried to break free from the leash until Gpa settled him.

The clerk couldn't have been much older than me. He had long, greasy black hair he kept tucking behind his ear as we spoke to him, and he didn't look any of us in the eye. I was pretty sure he was stoned, but I didn't care, because we paid in cash and he didn't ask for any ID. There were only eight bedrooms and two bathrooms in the cabin-motel, and we were the only guests staying there that night. The clerk said if we only paid for one room, we all had to stay in the same room. The owner would be there in the morning and she served breakfast at 8 a.m. Supposedly she made her own bread.

Corrina had had all the rest of our food from the taco joint bagged for takeaway, so we ate an early dinner in the kitchenette, reheating everything in the microwave, and shortly after it got dark Gpa went down to sleep. There were only two beds in the room, and that was almost all I could think about, and I wondered what Corrina was thinking about it, but just thinking about being in bed with her made me start to feel a little light-headed.

Corrina and I fiddled with our phones for a while after Gpa went to sleep. The common room had an enormous, vaulted ceiling with exposed log beams that rose to a point at the top of the A-frame roof. There was a fireplace with a flagstone hearth, and even though it was summer, it was much colder in the desert mountain night than it was in LA.

"Think we can get a fire started?" Corrina asked.

I was skeptical because (a) I'd never started a fire in my life and I immediately had visions of burning the whole cabin down and (b) I was paranoid that there was some rule I didn't know about that prohibited the starting of fires here and if we started one and got caught, we'd get kicked out. But stoner clerk had vanished while we were eating dinner, and Corrina was determined. She located a lighter in the kitchenette, but we couldn't find firewood. She stood by the stone hearth and flicked the lighter. I saw her shiver and I grabbed the big army blanket that was draped over the couch and threw it over her shoulders.

"That's nice," she said.

"So, are you really not going to call your dad back?"

She stared at the empty fireplace. "This is the line I remember best from his file on me," she said. "*She misreads reality easily, becomes confused, and becomes further confused by her emotions, unable to distinguish between different ones. This leads to disproportionate outbursts at other people, when, in fact, it is her own self-concept that is poor.* I don't really want to think about that guy, let alone talk to him."

"Man," I said. "That's rough." Oddly, though, it reminded me of Gpa, a diagnosis that probably fit him just as easily. I wondered what it would have said if someone had created a file on me.

"You know what the file doesn't say? It's not a tough one to figure out. But I'm serious, I have this feeling like everyone is always leaving me, or they're about to. And let me tell you something, Hendrix. They do. They leave. Well, fuck it. This time I left them."

She was quiet then.

"You know what?" I said. "I always thought you had a million friends, that you lived your life like a carefree rock star."

"Well, now you know. I'm nothing but Clusterfuck Corrina. Nice to meet you." She stuck out her hand, but I didn't take it.

"No," I said. "No, now I know that you're actually a lot more like me." I shrugged. "I'm not saying that's great, by the way. I'm just saying I get it—at least the feeling alone part."

Corrina wrapped the blanket around her tighter. "I really hate feeling alone, being alone. But I am. I'm really all alone, Hendrix."

"Well, me too," I said. "I feel like that all the time."

She shivered. I didn't want to sit there all night moping around, and because most of the light in the room came from dim lamps, I was reminded of the time Gpa and I had gone "camping" in the living room, back at the Great Empty Blue. It had been his idea, and I remembered it now with a kind of goofy nostalgia.

I sat Corrina down on the rug in front of the fireplace, and then I sat directly across from her, our knees almost touching. We tucked the corners of the blanket beneath us, and I held the center above our heads like a tent. "Flick the lighter," I said.

She did and the little flame danced.

"There's our campfire," I said.

"Wait." Corrina slipped out from under the blanket and ran to the kitchenette, and when she came back she had a flashlight. "This is better," she said. "For effect."

"It's like the metaphor of fire," I said.

"Yeah. Exactly, Poet. The metaphor of fire. Can metaphors keep you warm?"

"I'm not cold," I said.

"Me neither," she said. "Not anymore."

I held the blanket over our heads and she turned on the flashlight and put her fingers over the top and made flickering shadows on the surface of our "tent wall." She put the light under her chin and made funny ghost faces, and put the light under my chin and called me a zombie.

Then she held the tent above our heads and I took the flashlight and spun it in circles. "Look," I said. "It's the hullaballoo, those massive lights swinging in the sky above the theater on the opening night of your first big show."

She giggled and took the light back. "Look," she said, sticking the light in her mouth. "Maw sheek'sh on foi-ya." She took it out and stuck it behind her ear. "Now my ear's on fire." Her hair glowed a deep sunset amber in the light, and she pulled her hand through it, letting the strands loose, sending what looked like little sparks into the air between us in our tent.

"Be careful with that fire," I said. I took the flashlight from her again. "Look how quickly it jumps from you to me." I stuck it under my T-shirt, near my heart.

Corrina giggled. She reached up under my shirt and grabbed the flashlight. Her fingers weren't cold, but they sent lines of goose bumps skating across my chest. "Look," she said, doing what I'd just done. "It's happened to me, too." Her T-shirt was black and so the fire wasn't as bright, but it still sent something like another fire crackling down into the pit of my stomach.

"You know," I said, "I think I'm a better me when I'm around you."

"No, me too. Or, I mean . . ." She paused. It was dark in the tent, except for the light that rested on her chest. "I think I'm the me I want to be when I'm with you."

"Me too," I said.

It seemed like gravity was playing a trick or she was getting closer to me, leaning closer, the light coming closer.

"I just want to keep going," she said.

"Me too," I said. "I don't want to go back."

"Me neither."

"I like the way you say *neither*," I said. She said it with the long *e*.

"I like the way you say *neither*. Like you think you're British or something."

"Neither."

"Neither."

"Neither."

"Neither."

"Neither."

"Neither."

I could feel her breath on my lips, and even though I knew where this was going, I still think a simple question is always the best way to go, and there's nothing wrong with making sure the invitation is clear. "Can I please kiss you?"

And I know she was going to say *yes* because the flashlight fell between us and I felt that happy anxiousness stinging through me, and I just know we were about to kiss, but the front door suddenly crashed open.

Corrina gave a shout and I threw the blanket off us, wielding the flashlight like a dagger.

"What is this?"

A tall woman stood in the doorway with her hands on her hips. Despite the cold, she wore only a thin white T-shirt and a thin flannel shirt open like a coat. Rock-climbing ropes and carabiners were slung over her shoulder. She wore short soccer shorts and she was all muscle everywhere. Even her neck. She looked like she could pulverize stones if she tucked them behind her knees and did a squat. "What is this?" she said again in what sounded to me like a Russian accent. "Where is Greggie?" She was probably younger than Mom, but her hair was so blond it was white.

Corrina scurried backward and got up on her feet, and I followed.

The woman slammed the door behind her. "I don't run a teenage sex palace!"

"Umm," I said. "My grandfather is asleep in the other room?"

"You are having sex, with your grandfather in the other room?"

To be fair, I thought this was a better idea than in the bed next to him, but I didn't think arguing with Muscle Beach's Body Builder of the Year was a good idea.

"No one is having sex," Corrina said. She could barely lift her gaze from the floor and I could see the blush flushing her cheeks and neck.

"No sex! That is one of the rules."

"Are you the owner?" I asked.

"Yes." She stepped past us and went into the kitchenette. "Greggie!" she shouted.

"Please," I said. "My grandfather's asleep."

She frowned in response and went straight to the fridge and began pulling out food and creating a smorgasbord for herself, and it suddenly dawned on me that this wasn't a hotel at all, but her home, in which she probably ran an illegal bed-and-breakfast, and that was why they only accepted cash.

The stoner clerk came in from the backyard through the kitchen door. "Hey, honey," he said, lifting a lazy smile. His eyes were two red raisins.

"Greggie, did they pay?"

"Yeah."

"How many rooms?"

"Uh . . ."

"One," I said.

The Russian stone-crusher looked at Corrina. "Room number two. It's yours. Stay in it."

Corrina nodded.

"They have a dog?" Greggie said, his voice fading into his throat.

He had his hands in his jeans pockets and his shoulders

166

were hunched so high and so far forward I thought he was going to fold in half and close the book of his body on his own face. Just looking at him made me want to blink. For his sake.

"Breakfast's at eight," the stone-crusher said, not to us, but to Greggie.

"Got it," I said. There was an awful tension in the room and Corrina looked so mortified, but I was afraid to give her a hug in front of the sex police. "Hey," I said instead, finding a chirpy, cheery voice. "I hear you make great bread."

"I do," the stone-crusher said, still not looking at me.

"Well, good night," I said.

"Good night."

Corrina remained silent and I gestured toward the hall with the bedrooms. Her room was first and closest to the kitchen. "I'm not going to sleep a minute tonight," she said. "What the fuck is going on?"

"I don't know."

"I don't want to be alone."

"She'll kill us, or at least me, if she sees me come in with you."

"She's not looking." Corrina opened the door and stepped inside. "Come on," she whispered.

I hesitated. Bad idea. I didn't say anything else, I just paused out there in the hallway, and it was as if I said, *No. I can't*, or *I have to keep Gpa company*, or *I'm so scared I need my blanky-wanky*.

Corrina's face went still. She glared at me and then shut the door in my face.

I heard a knife chopping on a wooden block in the kitchen, and so, still clutching the flashlight, I opened the door to the closest bathroom and stood there listening until I heard the voices in the kitchen grow quiet and the bodies climbing the rickety ladder to the loft over the common room. I waited for a while and then stepped back out into the hall to go to Gpa's (and now my) bedroom, but paused again when I heard a noise in the common room. Then I continued quickly, and pissed off, because I was pretty sure what I heard was the stone-crusher and Greggie breaking the rules.

CHAPTER 16

TEST DRIVE

I woke in the morning as the only person in the room and panicked. I'd set my alarm, but obviously it was too late, and I leapt out into the hall and down to the kitchen without even looking at myself in the mirror.

Gpa sat at the table in the kitchenette, sipping a cup of coffee. I hoped it was decaffeinated. The stone-crusher was standing by the sink, sipping her own cup of coffee, listening to him tell her a story. She was smiling and looked happy and well rested and so did Gpa. He'd even put his clothes on and shoes, and with the exception of white grizzle on his cheeks and chin, he looked as sharp as I'd seen him in days.

"My God you can sleep in," he said when he saw me. It was seven thirty. "Asya tells me she met you two last night."

Okay. Weird. My mind was still partly asleep, but I knew enough to deflect. "Where's Old Humper?"

"Don't call him that."

"Your mind," Asya said to me.

"He's out back," Gpa said. "Greg's got him chasing down a Frisbee." He smiled. "Where's your friend?"

"I don't know. Is she up?"

"No," Asya said. She turned back to Gpa. "She sounds like she was a lovely woman, Charlie. You were a lucky man."

"I'm still a lucky man," Gpa said. "I still love her. And every minute I ever had with her was worth it."

I heard a door open behind me, then another one, which quickly slammed shut, and then the shower ran. I joined Gpa at the table and poured myself a cup of coffee. Asya cut a thick slice of bread on the wooden block and brought it over to me. "Zucchini," she said, and she pointed to the butter and jams on the table in front of me.

When she had positioned herself back by the sink she continued. "I try to tell Greggie this. It is not all wine and roses, yeah? You have to be a person of faith. You have to believe you two are right for each other and you have to believe you will make it work no matter what—you both do. Right? I am a person of that faith. The faith in me and Greggie."

"That's right," Gpa said.

I had my own thoughts about Greggie and what he might or might not have faith in, but I kept them to myself. I wondered how long they'd been talking and about what, and I feared it was a bad idea to stay somewhere people got to know us.

"I wish she could have been here as I've been going through

this Alzheimer's, though," Gpa continued. "She was my rock. She was so strong."

"Yes, she was," Asya agreed.

"How long have you two been talking?"

"Since six thirty," Gpa said. "Asya here is one heck of a hostess. Isn't this bread delicious?" It was, but I was more worried that Asya had called the police when Gpa wasn't looking.

They spoke some more, this time Asya telling Gpa how she and Greggie met, and I kept looking at the hallway, waiting for Corrina to join us. Eventually she darted out of the bathroom, wrapped in a thick towel, and slammed the door to the bedroom behind her. When she joined us in the kitchen, she sat across the table from Gpa.

She poured herself a cup of coffee and stared at me. "Hendrix, you stink like a sack of rancid onions."

Nobody said anything else for a moment.

"Good morning?" I said.

"Teddy," Gpa said. "Take that shower."

I was worried about what they would all talk about without me there, but I desperately needed a shower, and so I went to take one, but while I was scrubbing down the pits and trying to scrape all the rotten onion smell away, I couldn't help thinking that it was Monday morning, the day Calypso thought I'd be back with Gpa from the reunion, and only two days before Mom got back from Shanghai. If Calypso called her today, which they might, she'd call me and ask what the hell was going on, and I'd have to tell her what was going on, or lie, but I wasn't sure I could get away with it. I was so terrible at breaking rules—I didn't know what I was doing.

When I finally got back to the kitchen, wearing clean underwear and pink and flushed from the hot water and all that scrubbing with a hard bar of soap, Corrina and Gpa had the bags packed and stored in the car, and Gpa was sitting on a rocking chair on the front porch, waiting with Old Humper.

Asya was packing food with Corrina. "You're going to need this," she said. "Long drive today, if you plan to make it all the way to Oklahoma City." Corrina finished bagging the sandwiches and gave Asya a hug good-bye.

"I'll send you a file as soon as I can get it uploaded to a dropbox," she said. "Come on, Hendrix," she added when she turned to me. "We have miles to burn." She wasn't smiling at me exactly, but it was something like a smirk, and she breezed past me to the front door.

Asya took me by the shoulders. *This is it*, I thought. *Here comes the Judas kiss, the moment she tells me she called the cops and they're down the street waiting for us and why am I such an incredibly awful person who thought he could get away with this crazy plan in the first place.*

But she didn't. She mussed my now-clean and already perfectly mussed hair. "You are a good boy," she said. "You take care of your grandfather." She pulled me into a hug.

"Yes."

Then she released me and I could breathe again. "Now go!" she shouted, and I obeyed.

Once we were winding down the hill and on our way back out onto the highway, I finally began to breathe a little easier. Monday night: Tulsa. Tuesday night: Indianapolis. And Wednesday we'd have to make it all the way to Ithaca, if we could, before Mom figured out exactly where we were. And maybe, just maybe, I could hang on to the plan.

We were nearly at the junction to get back onto the 40 when Corrina said, "You know what stinks? I have to drive the whole time."

"I'm sorry," I said.

"Oh, man. You and your apologies."

"What can I do?" I said. "I am sorry I can't drive. I wish I could!"

"Hendrix, you have been beaten down by the rules so much you don't know when to think for yourself. That's sad, man. Sad."

"All right, pull over," Gpa said from the backseat. Corrina glanced at him and continued toward the highway. "Pull over," Gpa said again. She looked at me this time, and I nodded. She pulled over into the breakdown lane a couple hundred yards from the on-ramp to the interstate.

"Now get out," he said.

The car was still running, and Corrina put it in park. "Uh, Charlie, look. I hope you're not mad at me. I'm just trying to tell Hendrix here that he doesn't have to always be so afraid of things and follow all the rules."

"To hell with the damn rules. Get out of the car."

173

"Gpa," I said. "Don't get mad at her."

"I'm not," he said. "The two of you are driving me crazy. It's infuriating to watch! Now," he said to Corrina. "Get out of the car."

She did as he'd told her, and then he pushed the seat forward and began to climb out too. I jumped out of the car and ran around it to make sure he didn't stumble into the traffic.

"I'm driving," he said. "Teddy, get me to Tulsa."

This was a terrible idea. "Gpa," I said.

"I'm feeling great, Teddy."

"I know, but—"

"I drove this car more than your mother did when she first got it."

"Okay, but—"

"I've been driving my whole damn life, Teddy. It's second nature. And highway driving is the easiest."

A truck rushed by in the lane closest to us and the wind it threw against us blew Gpa's cap across the roof of the car. It wasn't close enough that it could have hit us, but close enough for me to imagine that it could have. I watched it veer off to the right and join the traffic on the 40. Corrina ran around to the other side of the car to get the cap, before it caught the wind and flew off into the sweep of pine trees curling up over the hills on the far side of the highway.

"Gpa," I said. "I know you can drive. But I can't let you."

"Teddy."

I took him by the arm, leaned closer, and whispered in his

ear. "Please let me do this. I need your help." I held on to his arm as I stood back. "Okay," I said across the roof to Corrina. "Teach me how to drive."

As soon as I said it, Gpa began to climb into the backseat again. "Thank God," he said.

"Are you sure?" Corrina asked. "You?"

"Yes."

"Okay, Hendrix," she said. "Let's do this."

Corrina drove the Blue Bomber to a huge, nearly empty parking lot in front of a Best Buy and a Home Depot, pulled into a space far away from the few cars that were parked near the stores, and turned the car off. We switched seats, and when I was in the driver's seat, Gpa leaned forward and patted my shoulder. "Nothing to it," he said.

"Okay," Corrina said. "Lesson one. Gas and brake."

She coached me, and Gpa did too, and after a few minutes of herky-jerky, slamming us into our seat belts and then back into our seats, I got the hang of the pedals and learned how to manage a fairly smooth transition, and then I got more comfortable steering and Corrina had me drive over to where cars were coming into the lot and had me merge with them so we could aim toward the store, and take a left, and after about an hour of all this, I began to feel a slight sense of what to do and Corrina urged me out onto the road, cheering, *Yeah, Hendrix, yeah,* getting me to accelerate until we came to a stop sign, and by some strange twist of cosmic fate the name of the cross street was Test Drive.

"Take a left on Test Drive," Corrina said, and laughed.

I did, pulling out a little too quickly and making the wheels squeal, and maybe a little too close to the oncoming truck that was coming at us along Test Drive, but even though the blood in my veins moved faster than the Blue Bomber, I felt good. The brown hilltops spotted with green seemed to beckon me, and the clouds in the bright blue sky were like cars in traffic above me, moving quickly and smoothly, some rolling past others and all of them heading back behind us.

We practiced for another hour on the roads around the neighborhood, until we came to a sign for Historic Route 66. It was an empty little two-lane highway running parallel to the 40.

"This is it, Hendrix," Corrina said. "Take it! All the way to Tulsa, baby!" She hooked up her phone and scrolled to a song and told me to step on it, and the music came on and she sang along with it, and I felt her voice moving through me, the dip and swing of her notes like the pulse of my blood, the hum of the Blue Bomber coming from the pedal and buzzing up through my leg, the crescendo in my stomach like the drop in my heart when she'd hushed and she'd breathed and she'd leaned toward my lips in the dark.

She belted out along with the song. I knew enough now to know how much she loved Patti Smith. I even knew the stats, like she did: "Because the Night," from *Easter*, 1978.

"Okay, all right," Gpa said from the backseat. "Teddy!" he yelled. "Slow down!"

I hadn't realized it, but I was pushing eighty and ripping past trees and meadows and the small shacks and the mud-wet gravel roads that curled off Historic Route 66. I eased up on the gas pedal and Corrina laughed and continued to sing along with the song, although she turned it down so we could hear each other without shouting.

When the song finished, Corrina went back to Gpa's playlist. "Sly and the Family Stone," she told him. "1969. 'Thank You.'"

He nodded.

"I'm still mad at you," she said to me, with one corner of her face pulled up in a smirk. "But you are all right, Hendrix. You are all right."

She leaned over and kissed me on the cheek, quickly and lightly, but between those lips was the entirety of the night before, and I was there again, alive and alert and alone in the tent with Corrina and the rest of the world in a still and quiet darkness beyond us.

"New York, here we come!" Corrina shouted out the window, her hair trailing in the wind, and when the historic route fed into the highway, I aimed the Blue Bomber east toward Ithaca.

CHAPTER 17

A SHORTCUT

We listened to: "Dancing in the Streets," "Think," "Route 66," "Mustang Sally," "Hit the Road Jack," "Ramblin' Man," "Going Up the Country," "Long-Distance Operator." Then Corrina switched the list and told me it was time to listen *only* to women who rock: the Ronettes, the Supremes, the Shirelles, Yeah Yeah Yeahs, Joan Jett, the Breeders, Heart, the Pretenders, Patti Smith, Bikini Kill, Melissa Etheridge, the Donnas, Flyleaf, Advaeta, Shingai Shoniwa, Cherry Glazerr, ZZ Ward, PHOX, Nadia Washington, Jessica Newry, and swinging all the way back to Dusty Springfield.

I drove us clear across the shrub-gray emptiness of eastern Arizona, and by the time we were passing what was called the petrified forest, although there was nothing to see except the same flat, endless expanse all around us, my mind kept playing tricks on me, because as I looked into what should have seemed like the infinite stretch of land around the 40, I kept thinking I was driving the Blue Bomber toward a fixed point where the sky and the land became one, as if I was driving dead on into the surface of an enormous canvas and if I got there fast enough I might break right through the threads and discover what I was looking for beyond it.

It was early afternoon as we approached the New Mexico border and lunar, multistrata buttes and enormous globular stone masses began to rise from the desert—lonely curved bodies stranded in time and empty space. The GPS told me that as we swung through the eastern reaches of Arizona into New Mexico, we were driving through Hopi, Navajo, and Zuni reservation land, and as I looked out at the small, square outlines of buildings almost floating on the crests of the wavelike hills, I thought about how far from other cities and towns these little homes were, how beautiful it must be to look out those windows every morning and see the world awaken over the desert expanse, but also how very distant the rest of the world might seem, and what that distance might mean.

Corrina's phone was our stereo always, sitting up on the dashboard in the dock, so it was all too easy to see when her father called, which he did, three times, and every time Corrina clicked his face off the screen, no interruption to the music, as if he couldn't break through the wall of sound she threw up in front of him. But after she ignored his third call, he sent a text, which, although she reached to flick it off the screen, I still read:

Don't make me call the police.

179

I was sure Gpa couldn't read it from the backseat, and I glanced at Corrina, but she looked out the window, away from me, and we didn't mention it. I watched her shoulders rise and fall as she leaned her head against the glass. I wanted to ask her about it, but I was afraid what Gpa would say if we clued him in, so I remained silent too. We didn't even talk about it when we stopped for lunch, but all I could think about was her father's threat, and that the police were already starting to look for us.

We thought we'd have to eat at KFC, Pizza Hut, or Long John Silver's, but we found a Route 66 Diner and decided that was the spot for us. Gallup was, at least at one time, called the Indian Capital of the World, but for two kids from West LA, the town seemed desolate and abandoned. In the small café, we saw photos of what must have once been downtown, brick buildings festooned with cartoonish signs, a junior-sized, cowboy version of Times Square, but all that was gone.

I wondered about that nickname for the town. I'd read somewhere that there are over five hundred different Native American tribes, each recognized as its own nation within the USA. It didn't seem right to lump them all together. Who'd come up with the name? It occurred to me that for most of my life, I'd seen images on the sides of mugs, on t-shirts, on school bulletin boards, at rallies, and on football helmets— team names, mascots, not the people themselves. I felt gross. We'd been driving across mostly Navajo reservation land, and I told the guy behind the cash register they should change the sign to GALLUP: A CITY IMPORTANT TO NAVAJO, HOPI, AND ZUNI POPULATIONS. CHECK YOUR GUIDEBOOK FOR MORE FIRST NATIONS CAPITALS.

"Uh-huh," he said, glancing at me briefly before giving me my change. "I'll try to tell somebody about that."

"You could," I added, realizing just how unwelcome my comments were. We got the food to go and ate in, on, and standing near the parked car in the lot.

After lunch, I offered to drive again, and Corrina didn't mind, because she was sleepy with a food coma after her triple stack of chocolate-chip pancakes. With her bare feet perched up on the dashboard and the seat tipped back, she fell asleep beside me somewhere outside a place called Continental Divide. She'd dropped a Gpa list back on: Chuck Berry, War, the Band, Aretha Franklin, Fleetwood Mac, Cat Stevens, Nick Drake, Neil Young, Jefferson Airplane, Marvin Gaye, Little Richard. The band America played over the speakers for Gpa at one point, and while he occasionally sang a few lines along with the song, I thought about how we were crossing this continental divide in the simple rise and dip and rush of the road, and how by that night we'd be four states away from one home and halfway across the country to another.

Eventually Gpa conked out too, and so when, shortly after we'd whipped through Grants, I saw a sign for a detour, I wasn't sure if it meant a detour was approaching, or if the route was a detour from somewhere else. Our road continued straight ahead, and the GPS told me to continue on the 40, so I did. But as the highway cut and swooped through Laguna Pueblo territory, I saw another few signs telling me to turn off the 40 and onto Route 6. Still the GPS said to go straight, and I did, rushing past the last sign that was posted just after the sign for exit 126 to Los Lunas. After we shot under the overpass, the desert spread out around us, or rather swept in, as only shortly ahead of me, the gray dust of the desert and the gray asphalt of the highway became one. All of it seemed to tip up and into the clouds.

I didn't see any other signs for a detour, but that made me more nervous. While the highway hadn't been crowded, at least there'd been trucks and RVs and a few other cars on the road with us. Now we were alone. And then, as the 40 bent a wide arc north and east, I saw the problem. The face of a butte near the side of the road had crumbled and buried the highway beneath a long slope of boulders, rocks, and gravel.

I slowed down and came to a stop in the middle of nowhere. There were no cars ahead, only the rubble maybe a mile down the road, and there were no cars behind. I thought about driving over the sandy median strip and doubling back to the detour sign, but there was another dirt road ahead of us, and I looked through the map on my phone and it indicated that the Indian Service Routes connected with Route 6, and I figured that would save time. After all, what had I learned in geometry class? The shortest distance between two points was a straight line. It seemed that was what the service roads were for.

I turned onto the dirt road, but after only a short distance the road became sandier and I had to slow down. At one point we hit a divot in the road and the bouncing woke Corrina up.

She gazed around us. "What the hell?"

Gpa piped up too. "What's going on?"

"A shortcut," I said.

"Oh, no," Corrina said. We hit another divot and the Blue Bomber slid sideways in the sand. "This is not good. What the hell were you thinking?"

"There's a detour," I said.

"This can't be it." Corrina cut the music and began playing with her phone to find a map. "Where are you taking us?"

I wanted to explain, but I was having more and more trouble controlling the car. The sand seemed to get deeper and the Blue Bomber kept fishtailing and bouncing. Gravel churned below us and splattered the undercarriage.

"You are a madman!" Corrina yelled.

Gpa and Corrina both kept yelling at me to slow down, turn around, and stop and explain, and I kept hoping I'd see some sign of Route 6 ahead so I wouldn't have to explain, so I'd show them I could get us there and get them both where they wanted to go, but as their voices rose and the car drifted and dropped and shook, I couldn't see anything but the vast, dry nothingness ahead.

Then we hit a rock and we heard a small explosion, and the Blue Bomber popped up in the front and slammed down in the dirt in a ditch at the side of the road. Everyone was silent in shock, until, with both hands on the wheel, I finally spoke. *"Fuck!"* I yelled.

I tried to go in reverse, but the wheels spun, and Gpa told me to stop. Despite how many times I tried to explain what I had done and why I had decided to do it, Corrina kept saying, "Detour. Detour. Can't you read?"

Gpa got out, and I thought he was going to survey the Blue Bomber for damage, but he wandered around back and walked across the road and stood there looking into the emptiness. Old Humper jumped out and followed him. Except for the lone butte way back in the distance, the rest of the desert was a wasteland of beige-burned dead grass and dust. There was nothing else to see except the sky and the ripped and tattered blanket of clouds above us.

PART II

Now

CHAPTER 18

The Problems We Can Solve

We live in three times at once: always in the present, but the past,
too, like our shadow trailing behind us, close on our heels,
and when we pivot, it spins with us, and suddenly it's our past
that's ahead of us, casting its dark outline over the future—
at least that's what it feels like to me as I pace in the desert,
thinking back to LA, and then turn, and with the afternoon
sun behind me, watch my shadow stretch out in front of me,
pointing east to St. Louis. I'm not sure I'll get there, but if I
do, the ghost waits for me there, but with another woman.

And now, as Corrina and I lean against the car and gaze into
the yellow-dry desert in the distance, I can't explain why I
feel this collision of memories, emotions, and expectations,
but I do not regret it, not even the ones that are boiling with
fear and anger. It feels okay to feel all this right now.

"Have you ever fixed a flat?" I ask Corrina.

"No. But it can't be that hard, can it?"

"No," I say, although I don't believe it.

We empty the trunk and find the spare and the jack kit under the lining. It doesn't look impossible. There aren't that many tools. But once we get down to it we discover that we're not sure if we don't know how to use the tools, or if the Blue Bomber is tipped too far forward in the ditch and we can't jack it up at this angle.

We're both sweating, and Corrina's held her hair back with one of her tie-dye bandanas, and she stands and walks away. "Hendrix," she says. "What if we don't make it?"

I know she's still mad at me and probably having second thoughts about coming on this crazy trip too, or at least having to deal with me and all my baggage. "What am I doing?" I blurt out, but then it all comes ripping out of me. "My mom is going to find out soon, and when she does she'll kill me, Calypso's probably going to ban me from ever seeing Gpa again, they've probably put out a Silver Alert, and your dad's probably called the cops already. What am I doing? Why did I think I could do this?"

I try to calm down and look out into the emptiness. The barrenness. The sun is still a blinding ball in the late-afternoon sky, and what comes out of me has the sound of anger but it's not, it's just free. "I'm just trying to give him something he wants and something no one else can or will. He's my Gpa, but he's all I have for a dad. Mom's always lecturing me about how important it is to be involved and do activities and meet people, and not once does she come to any of the things I sign up for. He does. Or, he did. And now look at him. It's not fair. I just wanted to show up for him for once. That's all!"

"Yeah, well, I'm here too," Corrina says to me. "It's not only your problem."

She's right, of course.

And she continues. "I don't know what I'm doing out here with you and your crazy Gpa either." She looks around. "I don't even know which way is LA and which way is New York." She looks into the sky to figure it out and points west, toward the sun. "You know, after my dad's calls and texts and all his pressure, pressure, pressure, I looked up the distance to Guatemala City. You know what's crazy? It's almost exactly the same distance from LA to Ithaca as it is from LA to Guatemala City. It's the same distance, and yet, what would I do when I got there?" She hesitates. "One seems so possible, and the other not." Her lip trembles. "I don't have an Ithaca. What am I supposed to do with that?"

She quiets and walks away from me, and I want to pick up a rock and bring it down as hard as I can on all the problems of the world like this one. Can you still love a person if you can't help her solve her problems? Are you any use to her at all?

I'm breathing heavy and I step away from the car because my body wants to do something, like smash something or climb a mountain, because everything that is in me wants to come out. It's the hot, suffocating press of the afternoon, and I'm so slick with sweat I wonder if this is how people dehydrate, actually feeling all the moisture dripping out of them, and I need a break. I need to walk away from Corrina and Gpa and Old Humper and wander on my own into the dust and see if I can divine anything at all in the tide of blood pumping in my veins or the scattered swirl of pebbles in the dirt. But there's nothing out there, and just as I think we really are coming to the end, and that I have failed Corrina and Gpa and myself, I see Gpa leaning down, inspecting the tire and the tools.

He holds the jack in one hand and the wrench for the lug nuts in the other and walks around the car. He opens the hatchback and sits on a wedge of space in the trunk. He's muttering to himself, and as I begin to worry what he might do with the tools in his hand, he beckons me, and then he waves to Corrina, too. At first she stares at him from twenty yards away, but then he calls her name, and she nods and walks to him.

"Look," Gpa says when we're all standing side by side again. "Let's fix a problem we can fix, and let's get back on the road, because we can't spend the night in the middle of the desert waiting for a miracle. We have to do something about this." He hands me the jack and Corrina the wrench. "Follow my instructions."

He directs us to the hatchback, where we sit and push, and press the back of the Blue Bomber more firmly into the dirt, then walk around to the ditch and do the same over the

189

front right wheel, then get the jack square under the car, close to the flat left tire, and he teaches me how to use the jack. I'm terrified the whole car is going to crash down on my arm, but it doesn't. He coaches Corrina as she twists off the lug nuts and hands them to me, and together, all three of us, we get the busted tire off and the spare on. Corrina gets behind the wheel as Gpa and I push, and after spinning in the dust and the dirt, the Blue Bomber begins to slide and crumble the bank of the ditch, and when the back two tires are set on firmer ground, the car climbs out of the ditch. Corrina reverses out into the middle of the dirt road and then stops.

We all tumble back into the Blue Bomber. Corrina turns and spins out and turns again, until we creep forward and cut wide arcs around the biggest dips and holes and rocks in the road. When we finally make it back to the intersection with the 40, I look back to see where we've come from, and it seems more like a cloud of dust disappearing back into the horizon line, and all I can think about is how scared I was that I had stranded us there.

We're quiet for a long while as Corrina takes us across the median strip and west on the 40, and it's like we're going backward, the wrong way, and time, that bastard, is really against us. Corrina doesn't seem mad as much as contemplative. She doesn't even have any music on.

"That was stupid," she finally says.

She doesn't have to say more for me to understand. "Yes," I say. "It was a bad idea. I was dumb."

"Wow," she says. "That was so easy."

"What?"

"You admitting that you were wrong."

"Of course it was easy. I'm wrong most of the time."

This makes her laugh. "You are dumb, but you are no idiot," she says. I like this. "Hendrix? One thing is for certain. You are a dumbass."

"Thanks."

"I'm just trying to figure out why I always like dumbasses."

"Are they all as dumb as me?"

She laughs. "Nope. You are the dumbest of them all."

I grin. "There's a poem for that."

She laughs again. "Of course."

CHAPTER 19

FATHER LOTUS

We take the 40 to Route 6 to the 25, and the Pan American Freeway into Albuquerque, where the late-afternoon sun fills the town with an orange-yellow haze. We look for a place to eat and find green-chili-smeared burritos and tacos in a giant diner called the Frontier, but we eat the food by the car again. By seven thirty we're back on the 40 heading east out of Albuquerque, and with Corrina behind the wheel and Gpa and Old Humper in the backseat, the music back on, the summer sun still hanging late into the day, and the road spinning beneath us as we glide across a froth of dust and concrete, we know we need to put miles behind us deep into the night.

But we have two problems. It is, after all, nearing the end of our third day on the road and we wanted to be much farther east than we are. I'd wanted to be in Ithaca tomorrow, but we're still making our way through the desert. We need to get road behind us, and the great wake of our route needs to bend north as we sail east.

"Can we drive through the night?" I ask Corrina.

"Maybe," she says. "If you sleep while I drive and then I sleep while you drive."

"We could be in St. Louis before noon."

"Yeah," Corrina says. "And we have to stop there."

"No we don't," Gpa says.

Corrina looks at me and frowns, waiting for me to respond, but I don't, because, in fact, I'm not sure I want to stop there. The thought of meeting her suddenly scares me, even though she's the one who can probably tell me about all the big stuff I want to know, and even more, all the small stuff I've always wondered. How did he laugh? Did he wear slippers? Would he hold the door open for strangers? Did he wash the dishes every night? Did he think wool was too itchy? Was he a pepperoni or plain cheese pizza kind of guy?

None of this is important, but all of it is, and it makes me think about all the questions Corrina has too. Goddamn it feels bad: I have my Ithaca, I have my St. Louis, too. What does it mean, if now, after all this, I don't go?

"We still have a long way before we get there," I say, and I'm grateful neither of them pushes back. Instead they let it go, for now.

For most of the ride, my leg has been a piston in the passenger seat keeping time with the rip and rumble of the tires on the pavement, but somewhere thirty miles or so west of Santa Rosa, as Corrina slows the Blue Bomber amid the thickening traffic and we eventually come to a stop, I find myself adjusting in my seat more, sitting up and stretching my back. I'm butterfly-pumping my knees. And we sit dead still for the entire duration of two Sleater-Kinney songs, before I finally explode.

"What the hell is going on?"

"I don't know," Corrina says.

"We'll move soon," Gpa says from the backseat. "Probably construction."

I keep craning my neck to see if I can find the beginning of this long line of traffic. I look at my phone and the GPS is useless. The highway is highlighted red for thick traffic, but there's no explanation, no signs for construction, no indication that there has been an accident or a tragedy and that emergency vehicles are on the scene.

Occasionally we inch forward, but we don't get more than a car length or two before we stop and sit again for a few minutes. Eventually I realize that cars are also backed up on the other side of the highway, but a mile or so down the road all the traffic on both sides circles the junction of the frontage road along the highway and a smaller road heading north. Many of the cars around us are as packed as ours. Kids around our age, some older. There are a couple of minivans and VW buses.

We sit for another song, and Corrina finally gets out of the car, leaving it running, and pushes herself up, one hand on the roof, one on the open door, so she can see too. She looks into the car next to us. "Hey," she says to the white kid with dreadlocks coiled in a bun. "There a show out there?"

"Yeah, man," he says to her. "Yellow Mountain Amphitheater."

"Oh, shit," Corrina says. "I've never been there. Who's playing?"

"Father Lotus."

Her face lights up. "He's awesome."

"Playing a double set," Blondlocks goes on. "Supposedly playing his entire new album for the first one."

"Dude," the driver of his car says, leaning forward and speaking to Corrina. "You should come with us."

"Wish I had a ticket," Corrina says.

"Look for a miracle," he says. "They happen." He cranks the volume in his car to what must be a Father Lotus song, loopy, electric, psychedelic rock, and the boys nod along.

Gpa has passed out in the back. He's snoring, and Old Humper's got his head in Gpa's lap. Blondlocks nods again, but he's nodding toward Gpa. "He can just hang out with the car at the village. It's cool. If I had a ticket, I'd give you one."

"Two," Corrina says, thumbing at me, and it feels like she just grabbed Blondlocks by the arm and flung him back to Arizona.

"Yeah," he says. "Right."

Blondlocks glances back at Gpa and then reaches into the glove compartment. He lights a joint and puffs at it while he listens to the music. The smoke drifts into the Blue Bomber. I'd like to think he's an idiot, like he's just waiting to get caught, but there are no cops, and truth be told, across the highway–cum–parking lot, little wisps of smoke drift up and out everywhere and disappear above the dusk-reddened desert.

We sit for almost half an hour and Corrina chats with the guys about Father Lotus's first two albums, and they love it because she knows way more than them. She declines the joint, twice, asks if I want it, playing cool-kid politics, but at some point, as Blondlocks takes a sip from his thermos and hands it to Corrina, she's not thinking. She's all caught up in her monologue about Father Lotus's signature layering technique, that whether it's electric or an acoustic set, he's a mastermind of orchestration. Blondlocks is rapt. He's listening to her like she's the opening band for the show, or it's the pre-show interview, the backstory that makes the concert even more exciting. He's just one of those guys who's happy and dumb, and too stupidly high to realize what he's doing, and his friend, the driver, isn't looking when Blondlocks passes the thermos, he only glances over after Corrina has stopped talking to take down a big gulp.

"What the fuck are you doing?" he yells at Blondlocks.

"That's disgusting," she says, passing back the thermos.

"Oh, shit," Blondlocks says.

The traffic begins to move and the driver whacks the wheel of their car as he rolls forward. He's talking to Blondlocks, but we can't hear because we haven't rolled up along with them. Corrina's just sitting there, letting the traffic move ahead.

"That was dumb," she says.

She lifts her foot from the brake and we roll forward and then actually drive because the cars on our side of the highway are moving now. "Are you okay?" I ask, because she's quiet, and it's not like her at all.

"I'm fine," she says finally. "Now. But I don't know what I just drank. I wasn't thinking. It was like iced tea, but it tasted like dirt and something else. Something like branches, or bark, and it stung a little. I can still taste it in the back of my throat."

We roll up beside the two boys again and Blondlocks is hanging out the window waiting for us. "Dude," he says to Corrina. "I should tell you that was cold brew."

"Cold brew?" I ask.

"Yeah," he says, as if that answers everything.

"It's fucking 'shroom tea, man," the driver says. "You'll be booming for hours."

Corrina shakes her head.

"Hey," Blondlocks says. "At least it's clean."

"Fuck you," she tells him.

"Hey," he pleads. "I was just trying to share."

"You're an idiot," the driver tells him. "An idiot." He leans over again, looking back and forth from the road to us, as both cars roll slowly forward toward the exit, following the rest of traffic. "Follow us, man," he says. "I mean, like, she shouldn't drive."

"I'm right here," Corrina says.

"You boomed before?" he asks her.

"Yeah," Corrina says. "Of course."

But of course she hasn't, and I can tell she's lying. He can too. "Just follow us," he says. "You'll need lots of water. And seriously. You can't drive."

Although I don't trust these two fuckheads one bit, I know I'll probably need more help than I realize, because although Gpa's still snoring in the back, he'll wake when we stop and I'll have two people on my hands I won't know what to do with. And Old Humper, as if he's read my mind, or, more likely, he's smelled the air of fear now heavy in the car, lifts his head and noses forward between the front seats as we follow their beat-up car and the rest of traffic onto the overpass and down into the darkening desert. As the sun sets, the clouds are wild swaths of violet and vermilion sweeping into the twilight sky.

Once we're off the highway, the cars move more quickly and we speed with the rest of them toward what looks like a crown of gigantic yellow rocks breaking through the earth and spearing up into the sky. The traffic spills into a wide lot at the far end of the basin. An enormous amphitheater is built up into the largest rocks in the crown: Yellow Mountain. Corrina would be excited. This would be a kind of paradise for her, but it isn't. I can see her trembling.

"Are you okay?"

"No."

"Is it doing something to you?"

198

"No," she says quietly. "I'm just scared."

"You should puke," I tell her.

"What?"

"Puke it up. Get rid of it. As soon as possible."

She looks at me, and I've never seen her so afraid. It's not sadness—it's a kind of fear I saw on Gpa's face when he made me promise, *Don't let me forget her,* the kind of fear that must come from knowing you've lost all control and something else is taking over.

"Pull over," I tell her. "Just pull over now." She does, and the two guys don't realize—or maybe they do—and keep driving. It's so much easier to pretend you care than actually put in the effort to do it.

Corrina steers the Blue Bomber into a little space between a couple of sage bushes and leaves the car running as she opens the door and runs behind one of the bushes, but it's barely a barrier. I get out of the car and try to give her the privacy to stick her fingers in her throat, but I want to be a reach away if she needs me. And then, as soon as I hear it I smell it, and I rush over and hold back her hair as the brown spray fizzes in the dirt. When she finishes, her face is puffy with tears, and she steps away from me.

"I'll be fine," she says. "I'm fine." She stops, wobbles, and plops down, stumbling into a sitting position in the dust. She stares ahead toward the back of what must be the stage. The amphitheater rises beyond it, filling with people already dancing along with the warm-up acts. Most of the desert around the stage, around us, within this whole half of Yellow Mountain's crown, has turned into a parking lot with a warren of streets between the rows of cars. People have set up little stalls in front of or behind their cars, and it is exactly like a village, as fuckhead #1 described it.

Between this pseudovillage and the stage, a giant, out-of-place fountain sends a column of water high into the air that dissolves in its own corona back down into the wide pool below. The multicolored lights aimed at the fountain make the water look like fireworks—but it is water, and that's what Corrina needs.

I can't leave Gpa on his own, so I head back to the Blue Bomber, turn it off, and wake him up. "What is this, Woodstock?" he says, and I can't tell if he, too, is in a different mind, the surreal delusions of Alzheimer's taking over, and it probably does look like what I imagine Woodstock looked like—half-naked people spinning in circles or rolling on the ground, clouds of smoke—but Gpa never went to Woodstock, so this is not a memory. He smiles and takes my hand. "Help me out of the car, Teddy."

I get him and Old Humper back over to Corrina, who, thankfully, did not get up and wander away into the desert night. Instead, she just stares at the fountain, listening to the music, watching the light show on the thousand faces of the crowd rising up the slope of the amphitheater.

"Corrina's sick," I tell Gpa.

"I see," he says.

She stands up, with my help, and I lead her over to the fountain, Gpa walking Old Humper alongside us, and just as we get there, there's a roar in the crowd, a ballyhoo of lights, and a surge of sound that seems to erupt right out from the center of the earth beneath us, and it must be Father Lotus's band, because Corrina starts jumping up and down, shouting, "This is what I want! This is what I want to do with my life!" and all I can hope is that she's talking about the music. But she steps into the fountain and runs around with her tongue out, as if she's drinking in the party-colored rain drop by drop. Old Humper chases after her. I'm freaking out that the cops will come, but there don't seem to be any—it's as if everyone has agreed to step away and just let this little oasis in the desert live outside the rules, outside time almost, a seething, writhing, chanting, throbbing mass of people with Father Lotus at the center of it all dancing, singing, and conducting the crowd of thousands like a mad, heavy-bearded priest casting out a pulsing web of music that rises up and blooms out over Yellow Mountain and us all.

For some people, this might seem like heaven, and maybe for a brief moment, it does for Corrina, too, but suddenly she stops, spins back around toward me and pukes again, right there in the fountain. Now she really pukes, and she falls to her knees, and I run in because when she falls, she goes face-first underwater.

I drag her out and sit by the edge with her as she heaves and heaves and nothing comes out, and then I help her wash her face, and she pulls me closer and I hug her with one arm and she hugs me with two, her head on my chest, and we stay like that, breathing, her head moving in rhythm with my chest, and I wonder if anybody else in the world feels like I do now, so free, so not alone, a word I fish for but can't find, but don't mind, because I know I'm living it.

We stay like that for a long while, and then, finally, she breaks from the hug and walks back over to Gpa.

"I'm sorry," she says to him. This almost makes me laugh, because I know that by saying it to him, she's also trying to say it to me.

"Sick, huh?" Gpa says. "You like this stuff?" he asks her, nodding to the concert, the last reaches of the light show from the stage and the fountain playing a faint kaleidoscope on his face.

"Yeah," she says.

"It sounds like something I've heard before, and also like something I haven't," he says. "It's entirely new, and yet it feels familiar."

"Yeah?" Corrina says.

"That's why you do covers, right? To make something your own out of what people thought they already knew?"

"Yeah."

"You're a good kid," he says to her.

"Yeah?"

"Yeah," he says.

He puts his arm around her and she accepts it and leans

into him, too, and while the Silver Fox might be cooler than me, I'm not jealous, because just like the parking lot out behind us is a kind of village, me, Corrina, Gpa, and Old Humper sure as hell feel like family out on the road together.

Gpa tells us we should head back to the car and dry off and look for more water to drink and as we walk back through the lot to find the Blue Bomber, there are people huddled around little gas stoves and fires, some people selling food—real food, nothing laced, like tamales and grilled cheese sandwiches—and bottles of water and soda, and we load up and talk to everyone else out there who's been hoping for a miracle tonight. There are even still a few doped-out loners wandering around with one finger in the air, but they're harmless, and I wish I had a ticket to give them.

Back at the car we eat our food and I make sure Corrina drinks at least two bottles of water and we listen to the music from the Father Lotus show. Gpa gets the ball out and plays fetch with Old Humper in the space between the rows of cars while Corrina and I sit out on the hood. Eventually they tire of their game and climb into the back seat.

"There's that saying," Corrina says. "'They always get you in the end.' That's true, isn't it?"

"Who?"

"*They,*" Corrina says with venom. "*They. They. They.* They're everywhere and they always win, and they always get you in the end. I've heard that before. And it's right. This world's not fair."

"Then what's the point of trying at all?"

"I don't know, Hendrix. I don't know. But I try anyway. I try because I think that's all I've ever really known." She glances at me. "I really hope Aiko calls back. A text, an e-mail, anything, man. I want into all this." She waves off toward the stage. "Not as a fan, as a real player. I want in."

"You will," I say. "Whether she calls you back or not."

I'm thinking about all the things I've heard Corrina say to me and all the things I've seen her do and the way I think her voice is as bold and necessary as the wind, as I look up at what are the brightest stars of the night. Mars, actually, a yellow-orange flash, and Spica, blue and bright and bursting against the purple twilight. The pair of them, rising ahead of all the others—Corrina's constellation, I think—her name in the marquee of the sky.

"I think that's what Gpa's always tried to teach me," I say. "To try. To believe, despite it all."

"I bet," Corrina says. "He loves you. He really does. You love him, too. It's a thing to see."

I look into the backseat of the Blue Bomber at Gpa. He's dozing. There's the faintest hint of a smile on his face, and I hope he's dreaming of Gma, dreaming of their old front porch, of the way her whole waist fit in the crook of his arm, and the way he would lift her, like that, with one arm, dropping his bag and lifting his free hand to the back of her head as they kissed.

"Corrina," I say as she looks out over the village toward the stage. "You're going to make it. You are."

"That's not what I'm thinking about now," she says. There are tears in her eyes. "My life is a clusterfuck. I don't belong anywhere."

I have no idea how to answer this without sounding like an asshole. How do I tell a person she does belong? That she belongs to her life, and her life—her self—is a good one? How do I say that? Isn't the whole point of belonging that you feel it? "You're not a clusterfuck," I tell her.

"They, they." She waves her hands in front of her face.

I take her hand in mine and begin to knead it. Her body relaxes and she turns her head to me. "Yeah," I say. "But none of it makes *you* a clusterfuck." I take a deep breath and try to say more. "I think there is a place where no one else belongs but us. Right here. You and me."

"And your Gpa," she adds. She smiles.

"Okay, him, too, and Old Humper."

She breathes through her nose and leans into me. "What are you even doing right now?"

"I'm massaging your hand. I did it for Gpa one time he started to go a little nuts at Calypso, and he calmed down."

"It kind of feels amazing."

"That's because you are literally tripping."

"No." She sniffs. "I'm not. Mostly I just feel exhausted, and a little disoriented. Like I've been awake for days."

But there in the moonlight and starlight and with the glow of Father Lotus's show on the rocks of Yellow Mountain around us, I begin to think about the campfire back in Flagstaff and how far we really have come.

"Corrina? Have you ever said 'I love you' to someone?"

She's quiet for a moment and I'm afraid to look at her, afraid to say what I really want to say.

"I don't know," she says, but from the tone of her voice, I know she has. "I mean, the ex-hippies, of course."

"Yeah, but . . ."

"I don't know. I thought I did once. Love someone."

Although I'm shaking on the inside I try to keep as still as possible on the outside.

"I don't know," she says. "For most of my life I thought I looked so different from my friends, I thought I was so different from everyone else. I look back, and I hate how much I wanted to be *pretty*. I didn't even know what I thought *pretty* was, but I wanted to be it, because I thought I wasn't it."

Her voice is so quiet and hushed and I feel so small in the enormity of the darkening desert around us, but still we're close again, like we were in our tent, and it makes me feel as large as I need to be in this world.

"And yet," I say, and take her hand, "you are, and that's not even what makes you so lovable."

"What does?"

"You can't have one part of you without all the rest. It's not about one part or another. It's the whole you."

"You know," she says, "at school, even those nights on the boardwalk, you were always so bent over, I was forced to stare at the top of your head, even though you're so damn tall. But now? Now it's like you've straightened up or some-thing. I can look up into your eyes. You have beautiful eyes, Hendrix."

This puts me on a rocket ship and I'm already hurtling way past Pluto.

"Can I please kiss you?"

"Kiss me?"

"Yes."

"The clusterfuck who smells like vomit?"

"Yes."

"You're crazy."

"Yes."

"Yes."

"Yes?"

"Yes!" she says, but then she reaches out and pulls me to her, and then we are really kissing right there on the hood of the Blue Bomber, right there with Gpa only a few feet away, which feels reckless and awesome, because it's poetry in all the best meanings of the word, the two of us giving the middle finger to the universe, our rebellion against the *they*, because even if *they* do get us in the end, at least we've had this, each other, and while no matter how loud we shout, the universe wouldn't hear us, or care, still we kiss and we kiss and we kiss and we know, however briefly, what it means to be alive.

But eventually, Gpa does make a little noise to remind us that he's there, and Corrina has to go find someplace to go to the bathroom, and then I do, and it's like everything is back to business, but I don't want it to be. I only want to be in that dream with Corrina.

When I get back to the car, I can hear her singing and playing her guitar a little distance away, and I find her in the road, walking circles with Gpa, singing a song with him, "The Dark End of the Street." I've learned enough by now to know it's a song by James Carr, but that Corrina prefers Cat Power's cover. She holds her guitar out in front of her as they pace and sing together and I know she's trying to keep him rooted and calm, as I'm sure, as the night winds on, he's slipped back into further confusion. *"Someday they may come along and find us alone somewhere."* I let them sing, and they drift toward me under the marbled light of the moon.

When they finish the song, she gives him a hug and he accepts it, and he tells her about the time he found Gma in the vegetable garden behind their house, hunched down in the dirt in her Earth Shoes, singing that song. Gpa had carved out the plot for the garden, chopped up the yard, dug a shallow trench, and filled it with rich soil. The story is already in the HFB. He told it to us earlier.

When they're back at the car, Corrina says to me, "I'm worried about driving on. I don't think we should go any farther tonight. I can barely keep my eyes open. I think I need to sleep."

"I think the world is already looking for us. There's no use in pushing on tonight. *They* might get us tomorrow, though."

"*They* haven't gotten us yet, Hendrix."

"What else can we do but try," I say. I smile and kiss her, right there in front of Gpa. He scrunches his face up quizzically, but then he relaxes. He nods. At that moment, I don't know where he is, or if he's actually with me, but somehow I believe that deep down we're exactly in tune with each other.

We settle Gpa in the front passenger seat and put the guitar in the driver's seat so we can huddle down in the back together. Old Humper tucks himself into the footwell with Gpa, and Corrina and I hold each other. We wait until we hear Gpa snoring before we kiss again, and then we stop, because she's too tired, and I just hold her in my arms.

We stay that way for a long time, but eventually she says very softly, "Hendrix, I think you might be my only real friend."

"Me too." I keep hugging her until her breath is calm and she is calm, and I realize she is finally asleep.

CHAPTER 20

CADILLAC RANCH

If you look at the state of Texas on a map, and imagine rotating the state clockwise so that what usually looks like its top hat is flipped to the bottom, the state will then look like a bird in flight, head held high, beak leading east—just as we fly east along the 40, turning time backward and upside down, our trip itself a kind of poem, making what was into what will be.

The next morning, after grabbing more provisions from the parking lot village, made up of all those who remain behind for the three-day show, we put Yellow Mountain behind us. As we speed east, the desert morphs from the mustard yellow of the New Mexican plateau into the green grassland of northern Texas, and the land sinks slowly into the wide basin of Middle America. It's not far after the dry and dusty creek bed of the Plaza Larga just outside of Tucumcari, New Mexico that we cross up and over one final rise in the road, and the last hill, mesa, and butte are behind us, and Texas extends into what seems like the whole rest of the country, an endless expanse of grassland. Heavy clouds gather all morning, and by the time we cross the border into Texas, the storms over the flatlands look like the limbs of an enormous beast loping across the desert. Lightning flashes in the distance. At first the road is still dry, the rain approaches from the north, its wet breath hovering at the edge of the road, waiting, but then the highway bends, and we drive straight into the storm, its smoky arms wrapping around us, pulling us in.

It is the road to Ithaca, the road to Gma, and the road to Dead Dad, too.

I turn back to Gpa. "Do you think my father loved my mother?"

Gpa blinks. He answers slowly. "He did."

"But what about later? What about when he was with the other woman?"

"It's hard to know," Gpa says. He shakes his head. "Once he had gone that far, I wondered if he could ever come back."

"But you weren't honest with me about him. She wasn't either."

Gpa nods. He looks back out the window. "We loved you, Teddy. We still do. It's confusing. Maybe you were too young to understand. Maybe you still are." He pauses.

"I don't think I am," I say.

"Maybe you aren't," he says.

A steam gathers tight and heavy in me like the rain clouds flattening the sky above. The world, maybe only my perspective, looks skewed, like the road ahead runs into the closing vise grip where the sky and the earth become one. It looks strange, and confusing, and yet I'm drawn to this unknown. It's like the old Greek myth, in which Uranus, the sky, and Gaia, the earth, join and from their love all life is born.

We're all quiet again, listening to Corrina's other playlist, the music she likes more, music from our lifetime: Conner Youngblood, Kimbra, Nick Hakim, Shakey Graves, Laura Mvula, Daughter, Lucius.

But then we see signs for something called Cadillac Ranch and Corrina asks me to see how close it is to the highway. The excitement in her voice unzips me. "I can't believe it," she says when I tell her it's right on the 40, a simple dip onto the Frontage Road for a mile or so and it's right there. Another mile down the road and we'd be back on the 40.

"We have to see it," she says.

"Why?"

"It's like this weird mecca for artists and musicians. We can't just ignore it. We're so close."

I shrug and agree to it. Somewhere in the back of my memories I feel like I've heard of the place before, but I can't call it to mind. Why do some things like words or images or memories or the answers to questions on tests hover just beyond recall in the mind? Why isn't every memory stored like a photo on the computer of my brain, and when I search for the file I want, it appears bright and clear in high definition instantaneously?

How much worse it must be for Gpa. What he can remember and what he can't. What he wants to remember and what he doesn't.

I look back at him as I've just agreed to another stop. It's Tuesday. Midday. I don't know if the time zone has switched or not, and I don't know what time it is in Shanghai, but I assume it's close to when Mom is packing for her flight back to LA; half a world away and still she strikes like thunder I can't hear and lightning I can't see, shaking me even in her nonpresence, but it occurs to me that some of the anger I feel toward her for keeping the stories of my father from me should also be reserved for the old man in the backseat, who stares out the window, watching the dirt turn to mud all around us. He's been quiet since breakfast and when Corrina pulls off the 40, guns it down the Frontage Road, and finds the gate in the barbed wire fence that leads to Cadillac Ranch, I'm trying to find the spirit that made me want to make this trip in the first place, but I can't. Instead, I want to do something for me. I want to spend time with Corrina, just the two of us.

Corrina parks near the fence, between what has become two puddles the color of milky coffee. Beyond the fence, a couple of hundred feet from the road, ten strange, particolored totems rise from the earth. It's a cow pasture, and in fact, there are innumerable black cattle grazing in the green field beyond the art installation. There's a sign on the fence:

STATE OF TEXAS PROPERTY
GRAFFITI
Painting of Anything
on This Side of Fence
IS ILLEGAL

And another one just beside it:

PRIVATE PROPERTY
DO NOT
TOUCH OR DISTURB
THE CATTLE

The signs are close enough to the entrance of the pasture that no one heading in could miss them, but as we walk closer, dragging Gpa with us through the muddy path toward the cars, it seems everyone has ignored this sign, because the ten cars, as they turn out to be, buried hood-first in the ground, ass up in the air, are all spray-painted in electric pinks, greens, yellows, blues, purples, and reds. They are all Cadillacs of the past; giant fins hug their trunks. I hold Gpa's hand as we get through the gate and begin to make our way toward them, but he's moving slowly and eventually I let go and stomp through the caramel-sticky ground to get to the cars with Corrina. I look back, and he's still making his way, and that feeling burns bigger and hotter within me and I just don't want to look at him anymore, I don't want to worry about him, at least for a while. I want a break.

Corrina tells me about how she first heard the Nitty Gritty Dirt Band's version of the song "Cadillac Ranch" but learned they were covering a Springsteen song. As she tells me more about this strange obsession she developed for the place, I find myself staring at the phrase *GB loves Brit*, glowing in a phosphorescent green on the roof of the closest car.

There are spray cans littered around the cars, all of which I assume are abandoned because they're empty, but I begin picking them up and trying them, seeing if I can make a mark of my own on one of the cars. Corrina joins me, there's no one else there, and we weave in and around the cars, trying can after can, until eventually I find a blue one with something left, and I step into one of the cars that has the door missing and spray onto what would be the floor of the car but is now an upright wall. I make two Vs with curls coming off their peaks, my abstract little birds, flying into the mess of color behind it. I can't help it. I have to show Corrina. She finds me, and she has another can in her hand. Yellow.

"Look," I say, pointing to my birds. "It's us."

"Where are we going?"

"I don't know, but I know we're going somewhere together."

"Which one is you?" she asks.

I point to the one behind, following the other. She grins and sprays an *H* beneath it. She sprays a *C* underneath the leader.

She's rolled the sleeves of her gray V-neck into the fake tank top again, and her shoulders are wet from the rain. I point to the spot where her shoulder meets her bicep. "Can I kiss you, right there?"

She nods, and when I do, she buries her lips in my nest of curls and kisses the top of my head, and we're about to make out, right there in the half-buried, hypercolored Cadillac, when Old Humper starts barking hysterically.

"Oh my God," Corrina says, stepping out of the car. "Where's your grandfather?"

I've been trying to trap my anger at him inside, because I know it isn't fair, but it's what comes out of me first. "Fuck!" But fear comes next and it's much stronger. "Oh, shit."

Old Humper barks again and again, and I find him deeper within the muddy pasture, closer to the cattle. At first I think he's playing a game, maybe, just trying to take a new role as herder, but I can hear the warning in his voice, and I know he's barking for me. Which means he's barking for Gpa.

Corrina and I run toward Old Humper. The cattle have moved much closer, and some of them must think we're bringing food, because they look up at us and start coming even closer. Old Humper now bounces back and forth, barking at the closest cattle, trying to redirect them, and as I get closer, I can see Gpa standing beside one of the cows. It lifts its head and turns, and when it does, it knocks Gpa down in the mud. We can't see him behind some of the other cows, and we keep running. When we reach him, he's just sitting there in the mud, looking into his lap like a child.

"Gpa, are you okay?"

He looks up at me in sad, frightened confusion.

"I can't get you home, if you stay out here in the mud."

"I've failed you," he says, not really looking at me.

"No you haven't. What are you talking about? I've failed you. I shouldn't have brought you out here. I'm sorry, Gpa. I'm sorry."

Old Humper barks, again, at another cow that comes too close.

"No," Gpa says. "No matter what you did, Jake. No matter what you do, those can't be my last words to you."

"Gpa, come on. You're okay. There are no last words here." But I know he's not talking to me. I'm not sure if he really thinks he's talking to my father again, or if he's just talking to himself.

"I should know better," Gpa says. "There's always grace. No matter what, there's always grace. I should have looked for it. I'm sorry. I'm so sorry, son."

Corrina looks at me. She's squatted down next to Gpa and she's rubbing his back. "What did you say to him?" she asks him, because she knows I'm too afraid to ask, even though I want to know. "It's okay," she says, holding him around the shoulders. "It's okay."

"'You're no son of mine,'" Gpa says. "'You're too selfish. You're no son of mine.'" He stares at the ground in front of him. "I'm sorry," he says. "I'm sorry."

Corrina keeps telling him it's okay and that it will be fine and that we should get him back into the car, and I want to speak, but the words aren't coming. Finally they do. "I love you," I say to him. "I love you, Gpa."

"Yes," Corrina says to him. "What about Teddy?"

"Teddy," he says, looking at her. "He's my only chance to make it right."

I am both there and not there in that moment. I am both the son and the grandson. The Prodigal Son, sort of, the one who's actually here and not supposed to blow it all for everyone else. But I am both the center of the world and a speck so small and so far from shore, the tide might carry me away. And this feels good—to have my own needs washed into the swell of Gpa's and Mom's. Like we're one family again.

"I want to go home," Gpa says.

"We're trying, Gpa. We're trying."

I'm not sure which home he means in the moment, but it sure as hell isn't a mud pit in Texas in which he drowns in his own guilt.

If there is any grace in this world, as Gpa says, I believe it is up to us to make it so.

Corrina and I each take a shoulder and lift him. We carry him out of the pasture, past the DayGlo cars, and Old Humper steps out ahead of us, leading the way back to the

Blue Bomber. The mud is everywhere. It covers our shoes. Gpa's pants and shirt are black with it. Corrina and I are both wearing shorts and the mud paints our legs with abstract globs and drips. Old Humper's heavy with it too.

But sometimes I think we find ourselves right there in the shit because we have to rise up out of it. *Try, because you must.* I keep talking to Gpa, telling him we've made it this far and that we're continuing ahead, and as I get his shoes off and begin to scrape the mud away, I look back into the pasture and think about Gpa doing this very same thing in the mud of Vietnam, a lifetime earlier, dragging one of his boys through the rain to someplace safer, telling him he'd make it home, because we can't give in or give up in this life when it's the only life we've been given—all for the grace of it all.

Corrina digs through Gpa's bag in the trunk for a clean shirt and pants, and I've got Gpa's muddy ones off and have him standing beside me so I can wipe out the backseat of the car, when a maroon minivan pulls up alongside the gate to Cadillac Ranch. Six kids around our age jump out of the minivan. They all wear the same baby-blue T-shirt, some youth group, and I see a man with the same T-shirt sitting in the driver's seat. He looks straight ahead at me and Gpa, and while I know it must look strange, I'm pissed he keeps looking. The kids stare too. They have to pass us to get to the gate, and they all giggle and snicker as they approach. Not one of them will look me in the eye, and no one asks if we need any help. I stand, try to make my body a screen for

Gpa, who's standing there in his underwear and T-shirt, and I'm trying to think of what to say to these gawking assholes, when Corrina pipes up.

"Hey!" she yells at them. "Have some decency!" She steps away from the car and waves them on with her arms. "Give the man his dignity!"

They rush past us and head for the gate, quiet as they go, but one of them bursts out laughing as they step into the muddy path to the cars.

Corrina hands me Gpa's nonmuddy clothes, the ones he wore on the day we left, and I set them on the now-clean seat. I dig out one of my own T-shirts and dump half a water bottle into it and wash Gpa's face and neck and hands with it. Corrina helps me get the clean guayabera on him and sit him on the edge of the backseat. He's still pantless, and I squat down in front of him and wash the clumps of mud from his ankles. I wash his feet. Gpa remains quiet and compliant through all of it, and I don't know if he's confused or tired or just raw like any person feels after a long cry, but he lets us clean him up and get him tucked into the backseat.

Old Humper's a mess too, but luckily he's a short-haired dog, and although the Blue Bomber's going to stink of him, at least he's relatively easy to wipe down. Corrina and I find another T-shirt and clean and dry him as best we can, and get him in the backseat with Gpa, just as the kids come back from their romp by the Cadillacs. This time they're quiet as they pass us, but still gawking, still speaking with their eyes,

We are us and you are them. The man in the minivan watches us the whole time—not like a creep, more with a lazy, bored look, as if he's too used to watching life on the TV screen instead of right there in front of his fucking face, where he might get off his ass and actually go live in it.

That's what I yell as they pull away from the fence. "Go live in it!"

Corrina laughs. "Okay," she says. "I guess we should get back on the road ourselves."

"Wait." I try to find a clean spot on the T-shirt in my hand, but there isn't one, so I take my shirt off and use it to wipe the mud from her cheek.

"Hendrix, are you giving me the shirt off your back?"

"Uh . . ."

"Oh, that's so sweet." She says this in a mockingly saccharine voice, but it's because she teases that I know she loves it.

"For you? Anything I can."

"You are nearly naked."

"True."

"Would you give me your shorts?"

I hesitate. "Like I said. For you? Anything." Then I smile. "I might be a bit cold, though."

She laughs. "Keep your clothes on, Hendrix, and drive us to Tulsa."

"Me?"

"Yes, you. And no shortcuts."

I get in the car, and Corrina gets in too, and she fiddles

221

with her phone for some music while I pull back out onto the Frontage Road.

"Charlie," she says. "Maybe this is one you like?"

Gpa's still quiet in the backseat, and even Old Humper's whimpering for a little attention. I wish there was a way to map Gpa's mind, to know where he goes when he's confused, or if he goes anywhere at all. *Meet him wherever he is,* Dr. Hannaway once told me. *Don't ask him to come to you.* As Corrina shuffles through her enormous database of songs, I know she's trying hard to find one that will help him, one that will mean something and keep him present and connected with the one thing he wants most now, Gma—at least his memory of her—and I think of how Dr. Hannaway's words are so important to the way I think about Corrina, too.

"I'm Your Captain/Closer to Home," Grand Funk Railroad. 1970. *Closer to Home.* Gpa begins to sing along with the song, softly, more saying the words in his squeaky voice than actually singing, but mostly staying with the song. The lyrics repeat and repeat and gather momentum, but somehow they also tell a story, which, of course, I like too. But Gpa fades. He doesn't stick with it. The words sputter, as if he's swallowing some; the lines are half broken. *What happens in a mind like that, I wonder, the world a window with rock-punched holes and the jagged pane still standing?*

We're back on the 40, sailing toward Amarillo's small skyline, as I think about this song that's playing, a song I now know is pretty typical in its rhythm, blues infused, a rock anthem that builds on the repetition of the lines, as the stanzas repeat the way sometimes lines do in poems. Gpa knows the words because he's heard them so many times, but he can repeat the words because of the rhythm, the pulse, the music in the lines. As the song builds and as Corrina sings along with it, hoping to lift Gpa with her, I think about what it would be like if I wrote Gpa a song, or a poem, a poem with music and repetition, something he could tap into, one poem that tells the story of him and Gma, something he could repeat for himself like a record that keeps on spinning and never comes to the end.

CHAPTER 21

What I Know About the Truth

The rain eventually stops and the clouds begin to break up as we put the Texas Panhandle behind us, and halfway through the state of Oklahoma the toll roads around Oklahoma City force us to zig and zag and slog along the small routes up and into Tulsa. It takes longer, but we do it, and the only real complication is finding a place to stay. We need showers and beds and a place to keep Gpa quiet and calm and settled. Nobody wants a dog, or if they do, they'll only accept a credit card payment, which we can't do, because if Mom has spoken with the folks at Calypso, she knows something is up. If she's checked our joint account, she's put two and two together because I withdrew as much cash as I could when we were back in LA. If she's come home early and found the Blue Bomber gone, the Great Empty Blue even emptier, and even Old Humper vamoosed, she's looking for us right now, and so are the cops, and because we've made it this far, we can't give in now.

But then one of those fears comes true as if I've called it right into the car. My phone buzzes and it's Dr. Hannaway. I let it ring, the phone just buzzing and bouncing in the plastic cup holder between the front seats, and Corrina glances at me, and neither of us says anything, because we both know we don't want to alert Gpa to it. I pick the phone up and listen to the message, keeping the volume low so only I can hear it: *Where are you and where is your grandfather? We're communicating with your mother, and we know the truth. There was no reunion. Contact us immediately.*

But she's wrong. She doesn't know the truth. It is a reunion, sort of, and it's just taking us longer than I thought to get there.

I know the road points east again when the sun sets the rearview mirror ablaze as it sinks into the prairie land behind us. I miss the name of the river, but as we cross it, a flock of small birds shoot out from beneath the bridge, rise, and fall again like dark stars in the dusk. Corrina uses her phone to find a duplex where the guy rents out the bottom apartment. Cash up front and it's ours.

It takes a while to actually find it, but we do, block after block after block of brown, slat-sided, look-alike two-story apartment buildings all corralled behind a black iron fence that runs around the entire complex. The owner has a lumber-jack's beard and boots with the laces loose, but he's wearing shorts. He meets us in front of his building. We swap cash for the key.

"Any rules I should know about?" I ask him.

"Rules? Why? Do you need any?"

Corrina laughs. "No," she tells him.

He looks at me. His eyes are set deep in his head and are almost black beneath the crow's wings of his eyebrows. "Where are you from?"

"LA."

"Where are you going?"

"Ithaca."

"That's one hell of a road trip."

"It's true," I tell him. "And everybody respects the road trip, right?"

"Kick ass, man," he says, and slaps my palm and twists and clenches my hand in a shake way too cool and hip for me to understand.

"Badass," I say.

He nods in agreement. "Just strip the sheets, dump them in the washing machine, and be gone by ten," he says, and then flashes us the peace sign before climbing the stairs to his own apartment. Corrina-like power chords reverberate into the parking lot when he opens his door and are gone again when he closes it.

We get Gpa inside, and I find *SportsCenter* on the TV, hoping to get him some baseball highlights. The ceiling's low, the kitchen and living room are really one room with a see-through bookshelf dividing them, and there's only one bedroom, but the couch is a futon, the bathroom is spotlessly

226

clean, and the place is cheap and ours. There's even a washer and dryer in the kitchen closet, and Corrina asks me if I'll take care of our clothes while she makes a run to a store for some food.

"Just don't get locked out for the night," I tell her. "Looks like this place has some serious curfew."

"Are you worried about me, or worried about breaking the rules?" Corrina says, and yes, I'm a dumbass, because I don't realize she's teasing until she closes the door behind her, but I know I'll be counting the minutes until she returns.

As I get the laundry together, Gpa comes alive watching the sports highlights. It's all baseball, and Gpa has a complicated matrix of teams he roots for, including the Dodgers because they're previously from Brooklyn, transplanted from New York to LA, just like him, and he's happy because they won yesterday.

"Gpa," I say behind him. "I'm going to put your bag in the bedroom."

"No." He speaks to me while still watching the TV. "The room goes to the girl."

"I think Corrina would rather you have the bedroom."

"Me? Where do you think you're sleeping?"

"Uh..."

"We'll camp out here," he says, gesturing to the room around us.

I have no idea what Gpa thinks is going on between me and Corrina, or even what he thinks about dating and hooking up or any of this. We've never discussed it in depth. Who talks about sex with his grandfather? But that is what I'm thinking about. That's all I'm thinking about: Corrina will walk back in the door, we'll make dinner, we'll put Gpa to bed, like a child, and the two of us will finally be alone again.

"Why don't we talk about that after dinner," I say.

He lets out a mocking laugh. "Right."

"Hey, Gpa," I say, trying to change the subject. "There's something else on my mind." And it's true, it's been sitting there like a grenade, and once I release the handle I won't have to wait long for the boom. "What's her name?"

"Your friend? Corrina? Don't test me like that."

"No, the woman in St. Louis. The woman from Ithaca."

Gpa sighs. He switches the TV to mute and turns in his chair, away from the TV, to look back at me. I'm sitting at the little round dining table, and the only light in the room, other than the TV, is the flat UFO globe that hangs above me. He probably doesn't know what he has said and what he hasn't said to me. I feel bad for him, I don't want to play with him, but I can't stop.

"The whole story, Gpa. I need the whole story."

"Teddy, I'm sorry. I don't know the whole story."

"No," I say. "Not good enough anymore. I need more than the usual script, Gpa." I know it's mean, but there's something like a wave breaking in me, the crest of it finally falling and foaming. "Why did you say that to Dad? What was he doing there?"

Gpa gets up and joins me under the UFO. He's slow, and he wears the day like a wet coat on his shoulders. "CC," he says. "Cecelia Devons, but everyone called her CC. I knew her." He rubs his face. "Listen," he says. "This is what I know."

THE STORY OF
DEAD DAD'S FINAL DAYS

Cancer snuck up on Gma, and when she was diagnosed she wasn't given more than a year to live. I was in school, so Mom stayed home with me, but Dad started making trips back to Ithaca to spend time with his parents. At first it was once a month, but then, sometime in the spring, he started going out almost every week. That was what he told Mom—he was going to see Gpa and Gma. Most of the time he was, but, as it turned out, not always.

Sometimes, if he was only coming out for the weekend, he didn't tell Gpa, and on one of those trips, one evening, when Gpa was walking down Mulberry to the hardware store, he took the short-cut, the alley behind CC's Café. He wasn't looking ahead, only down at his feet, lost in thought about Gma and how little time she had left, when he stopped a few feet from the steps out back behind the café's kitchen. He didn't believe it at first, but there, under the pale back-door light, his son, my dad, sat on the steps kissing CC herself—the woman Gpa used to buy coffee from before he and Gma had given up coffee, a woman he knew because she'd gone to high school with Dad.

There, under the dim, one-bulb light, it wasn't difficult to guess what was going on. CC and Dad were both wet with tears. They were kissing with the passion of people who knew each other well, one of Dad's hands holding CC's, the other gently resting against CC's cheek. Gpa had had no idea Dad was in town. A friend had said he'd seen Dad in town two weeks earlier, but Gpa hadn't believed him. Dad hadn't visited Gma then, either.

"How dare you," he said to Dad.

Dad jumped to his feet and tried to explain, but Gpa cut him off. "Your mother is dying, and this is how you treat her? Your wife is at home with your son, and this is how you treat her?"

Dad stepped forward, but Gpa pushed him back, and Dad tripped on the steps. "I'm calling your wife, Jake. I'm calling her to tell her why you are no son of mine."

He stormed off, not to the hardware store, but back home. Where he called Mom and told her what he'd seen, and what he knew now was an affair Dad was having with CC Devons.

Dad's car broke through the railing and sank to the bottom of the river that night.

"Your grandmother died six weeks later, and your mother invited me out to LA to help her raise you. 'None of us need to be alone,' she'd said. 'I'll take care of everything.' She's a remarkable woman, Teddy. Your mother. She reminded me of your grandmother."

When Gpa finishes he's quiet, and I am too, because the features in the ghost of Dead Dad's face have become clearer. The crinkles by his eyes and the lines in his forehead come into focus, like he really was alive once. This is not a man I'm proud of, not one I want to boast about, but he seems more knowable, and I'm glad. When he died, I was robbed of a kind of future—but what would it have been? Gpa, I realize, was robbed of a past—a whole story wiped out by guilt, not the disease, and I wonder what this has done to him.

"I'm sorry," I say. "Does it hurt to remember?"

"Yes," he says. "But I'm glad. I'm glad to remember him."

I get up and give Gpa a hug.

When Corrina gets back, she finds us hugging, Gpa in the chair, me down on one knee on the rug, and she doesn't say anything. She closes the door behind her with her foot and carries in the bags. I jump up to help her, and we unpack in silence. Grapes, bananas, milk and cereal for the morning. Road snacks. Three microwave dinners. A pint of ice cream to split for dessert. I warm up the dinners, while Corrina sets the table and Gpa hangs haggard in his chair. When she's close to me she asks what's the deal.

"I'll tell you later," I say.

We sit down to eat. The TV's still on, and I think about taking it off mute, just to give us something other than our thoughts to hear, but Corrina beats me to the punch. She finds the remote and the three of us sit there quietly while the sportscasters do everything they can to muster our enthusiasm.

Instead, after dinner, we do dishes. We take care of the laundry. In the quiet, easy pace of the night, I think about the poem, and lines begin to form in my head: *Anyone can fall in love, it's the staying in that matters.* This is important. I don't want to half-ass it. I want this poem for Gpa.

After we unfold the couch into a bed, Gpa declares again that the bedroom is for Corrina and says he and I will share the couch. I protest again, but Corrina doesn't battle with him. Instead, she rests her hand on my back and says, "I'll take the bed." She rubs my back as she says it, and I agree, because I'm a numbskull and only now understand why Corrina has been smiling at me as we've been doing all these silly house chores. Actually, not so silly. They felt real and somehow meaningful, as I stood next to Corrina while doing them.

Corrina heads to the bedroom to put her clean clothes back in her bag, and shortly after, Gpa's finally asleep, passed out on the futon. I pull the cover up over him. I lock the

front door, lock the deadbolt, too, knowing I've been waiting for this moment all night, and wondering if Corrina has
too. I turn off the TV, and the only light now comes from
the bedroom door, which is only slightly open, and even that
light's not much, it's only what comes from the lamp on the
bedside table.

I walk over to the door and whisper her name. She whispers mine back, speaking into the narrow space left by the
door standing ajar, and although I can't see her, she's right
there on the other side of the wall, as if she's been waiting
for me.

"I'm not tired."

"Me neither."

"Neither."

"Neither."

"Neither."

Her hand appears and floats slowly out from the room.
It finds my face, her fingers on my cheek, her thumb on my
nose, and then she drags one finger and places it on my lips
to silence me. "Shhh," she whispers. "Get in here."

I step in and she closes the door behind me quietly. She's
changed her clothes. She's wearing a pair of my boxer shorts
and one of her own faded gray T-shirts, and there is a lump
in my throat so tight I'm sure it's going to make me cry, and
what kind of a miserable, pathetic dumbass cries in front of
the most beautiful girl he has ever known just before he asks
her what he needs to ask her.

"I can't talk," I frog-whisper.

"Then don't."

"But can I kiss you?"

She rolls her eyes and waits before she answers. "Well, yes, Hendrix. Yes you can. Please do."

Then we're really at it, standing at first, but I feel so weak-kneed and nervous, I have to sit on the edge of the bed, which makes her taller than me for a bit, as we continue to kiss, but then she pushes me back and she's on top of me and her hair's down on my chest, and I find with my fingers the soft groove behind her ears, and when we need air, we roll on the bed and laugh, and suddenly both look toward the door. We listen. Nothing. We return to each other, quietly and softly.

"Slowly," she says.

"Okay."

We fumble with clothes, and the sheets are cool on my shoulders and back. "Can I kiss you here?"

"Yes."

"Can I kiss you here?"

"Yes."

"Here?"

"Yes."

"Yes?"

It's all whispers, but I listen. I listen with ears, I listen with my hands, I listen with my body, and I lose track of time as I listen to the language of her drawn-up knee, the space she makes for my hand behind her back.

"Do you have a condom?"

My eyes are closed when she asks, and I keep them that way as I answer. I feel so stupid. "No."

"It's okay," she says. "I got some at the store."

My eyes are still closed as she pulls out the drawer beside the bed, but I have to open them when she places the foil square in my hand.

"Have you ever had sex before, Hendrix?"

Doesn't every boy want to lie when he's asked this question? Doesn't every boy want to be more the man he wishes he was than who he actually is? Camp. Doesn't everybody find a story to tell about how they had sex at camp or somewhere like that? *There was a girl at camp, yeah, you can't know her because you weren't there.* Yeah, foolproof. Camp. Yeah, I got laid at camp.

But no, not with Corrina. The most important truths aren't the ones you learn but the ones you tell so the person you care about most knows too.

"No."

"Can we?" she asks.

"Yeah."

"I just thought I'd ask."

She smiles and it breaks open the night like moonlight on the water, one source bursting into a million little brights, and my body feels like the long side of an iron bell struck by her breath so close.

CHAPTER 22

BONNIE AND CLYDE

I wake in the morning from a nightmare, or rather, I feel as if I haven't slept but dreamed awake, floated right on top of sleep, aware of dawn and the brightening morning in the pale blue line of light around the window shade in the bedroom.

In the nightmare, Dead Dad is alive in a house in St. Louis. He watches me approach from a distance, his face a blur behind the window screen. It is a dream, and the screen has elasticity, and he presses forward, first his nose, then his chin, the mesh outlines of his face like an ancient death mask. Then I am on the porch. I am beside the window. I am hiding. I don't want him to see me, but the gray face turns, there are no eyes, but even without them he sees me. I run but his voice follows me like smoke.

It's so early Gpa isn't even up yet. I still lie under the sheets beside Corrina, and I don't think either of us has really slept much. I can hear her breathing. I don't want to get up. I don't want to go anywhere. I want to stay in bed with Corrina and find a way to slow time and pretend the rest of the world isn't moving around us, but it is, and Gpa's right there on the other side of the wall, and like all Gpas he's an early riser, and I can't stand the guilt that has crept up on me so quickly.

"I should get back out there," I say.

"Yes," she says, and despite how I feel about Gpa in the next room, and how that makes me feel wrong, I also can't help feeling like I've done something right. *Yes*, she said last night. *Yes*, I said too. *Yes. Yes.* I feel like I'm actually living.

Once we're all up and showered, we have breakfast together, and although Corrina and I don't talk about the night, we can't help but dodge, catch, and run from each other's glances, and I do everything I can to keep another conversation going.

"It's Wednesday," I say. "We need to make it to Ithaca by tomorrow. Nine and a half hours today and nine and half hours tomorrow, and we're there."

Corrina studies the map on her phone. "Indianapolis today, Ithaca tomorrow."

"Yes."

"Yes," she says, looking up at me, and neither of us can keep the smiles from rising on our faces.

Gpa watches us.

We're on the road again by eight thirty, but getting out of Tulsa without taking a toll road is tricky, and we're forced to take the narrow, two-lane Route 66 again, and this time with much less enthusiasm. We move so much slower today, as if we can't stay apace with the world around us, as if the Blue Bomber remains motionless and the world spins and spins beneath our tires. I want to get there. I feel close, and yet still so very far away, and our pace makes everything worse.

It takes three and a half hours just to get to Joplin, Missouri, which should have taken less than two, and at this rate we'll never make it in time. I've turned all the notifications off on my phone, so I don't know when any messages come in, but I check after we pass underneath the 44 yet again, and I shake my fist at the concrete bypass overhead, the damn toll road and its cameras. They haven't caught us yet, but as I check messages, there's one from Dr. Hannaway at Calypso: *Teddy. Please call. I just want to know that your grandfather is safe. He's going to be frightened, Teddy. He's going to be confused. Please go to a hospital. Go somewhere safe to turn yourselves in. There are other branches of Calypso. Are you near one? Go to it. Don't wait. The police know. We're talking about the police here, Teddy. This isn't a game.*

They issued a Silver Alert as soon as Mom called to let them know Gpa wasn't at the Great Empty Blue, as she explained that I was gone, Old Humper was gone, and so was the Blue Bomber.

Only a few minutes later I have new messages from Mom, too. She's texting. She's not even calling.

On way to airport. Leaving Shanghai early.

238

Spoke with Dr. H.

What the hell are you doing?

Some time passes, and a fourth one arrives:

Are you ok? Just tell me you are ok.

We pull in to a Snak-Atak to get gas and I walk next door to the Trading Post to find us something more than a bag of chips for lunch. I find a few wilted, colorless sandwiches wrapped in plastic. When I get back, Corrina has pulled the Blue Bomber away from the pump and parked it beneath a stand of elm trees. Throughout the drive today, I realize, we've seen more trees than we have since we left LA. And they're different here, like the air gets between the branches more, there are more leaves and in the light breeze the branches bow and wave independent of each other, like a clustered crowd of people all dancing independently together.

Corrina, too, is on her own. Gpa has Old Humper on the leash by the blue Dumpsters in the back of the lot, while Corrina sits on the hood of the car, staring at her phone. She's in her black jeans and she's wearing a black T-shirt with a large white blow-up of the parental advisory silkscreened on the front. The sleeves are rolled, as usual, and I can't see her eyes behind her sunglasses, but I know, from the weight in her cheeks, there's sadness there.

When I go to her she tells me she's reached out to Aiko. She hasn't heard back yet, but she's hoping for a text, an e-mail, a call. Something. Anything. Just a hint that something

239

waits for her, somewhere other than LA, her parents, and Rosewood.

"I feel like I'm really running," she says. "Like I don't want to go back, but I don't know where I'm going, either."

I nod.

We're on the outskirts of Joplin, Missouri. This is Mark Twain country. This is where Bonnie and Clyde stayed for so long, shortly before they were caught. "We're fugitives," I say.

Corrina poses by the front of the car and we take pictures. She gets her guitar. She holds it out, Johnny Cash style, she says, but it looks like she's holding a gun. We are fugitives. I get in some photos with her. I try to look dangerous, but I don't. I look scared. I am scared. Corrina looks badass, like usual, but she's scared too. She's just better at hiding it than me. She has more practice. I wonder now if, somewhere deep within her, she's always been as scared and anxious as I've been.

I walk out away from the trees, closer to the road, where the signal seems slightly better to send her the pictures like she asks, but then, because I'm still thinking about what Gpa said about Mom last night, and I feel bad she's left Shanghai early, and I know there are so many people worrying back in LA, I send Mom a text:

We're fine. Don't worry about us. I'll tell you everything when you get home.

And then it hits me, as soon as I press Send: We are going to get caught. Just like Bonnie and Clyde. I turn my phone off.

"Corrina."

"Hendrix."

"GPS."

"What?"

"They can track my phone. The police. They might know exactly where we are. We need to go. Now."

Corrina starts the car while I get Gpa and Old Humper, and when we're all back in the Blue Bomber together, we zigzag over to Route 60 and take the small road out of Joplin toward St. Louis. We can't get on the highway at all, where the state police patrol. Our license plate must be in the system now. They have some sense of where we are, and I wonder if Mom has given them any ideas of where to look for us. I wonder if she's figured it all out, if she's flying directly to Ithaca from Shanghai and she'll be waiting for us on the porch as we pull into the driveway of a house none of us even know is still there or looks the same as it did when Gpa and Gma lived there.

Corrina drives as fast as she can without driving too fast. We can't get pulled over. We can't get caught now. Not yet. We just need another day or two. That's all I want.

CHAPTER 23

WHAT WILL I DO NOW?

Our new back-trails route takes us into Mark Twain National Forest, and it's long after the trees have enclosed us between two green walls that I realize that for the first time since we left LA, we're driving without a view, without a sense of the horizon line, without being able to see what was behind us and what's ahead. The road winds deeper and deeper into the forest and there's no way of knowing what's around each bend. Occasionally we pass a house, or the pieces of a house, alone and crumbling in what feels to me like the middle of nowhere.

But as the forest begins to break up around us a flat patchwork of farmland and grassy meadows opens up around State Highway P, the one-lane road that carries us. The landscape reminds Gpa of the fields around Ithaca. He hums a little and smiles in the backseat. Corrina and I stay quiet as he begins another story, and I'm glad I don't have to jog his memory, or even ask him to think about it. The story just comes out.

THE STORY OF GPA FINALLY COMING HOME

Gpa had made the cross-country trip in this direction before. After surviving Vietnam and finally making it back at the end of his second tour with only time left in the reserves, he got to San Francisco, made his way to the bus station in Oakland, and took the six-day trip to Cheyenne, Salt Lake City, Omaha, Chicago, Cleveland, Buffalo, and finally to Ithaca.

He made it and he was home, and he and Gma sat on the porch staring at each other, trying to find words. Gpa intuited what the sweaters were for and reached for Gma's hand. "I'm home," he said. "I don't have to go back." She knew some figures. The war was all about figures these days, body counts on the news, number of villages reclaimed, budget numbers, vote counts in Congress, but the figures she knew were about days, all 786 of them since he'd left for basic training. But now he was home.

As they sat on the porch, all Gpa could think about was a similar porch on a similar hill in town where they'd sat six years earlier and begun what they'd called their nondate the night they fell in love. And as they sat there holding hands, Gma eventually told him what she feared the most. "This isn't going to be easy."

"I know," he said.

And it wasn't. Everything was different. It was April 1969, and Ithaca was not the same as when he left. He couldn't figure out what was what. Everything was different when he got home from the war. The clothes, the way people talked, their strange air of ironic bitterness—didn't matter what they believed, what their politics, to Gpa, everybody now acted like a know-it-all. He had a hard time adjusting. He fell out of bed at night with night-mares chasing him to the floor. He punched a hole in the kitchen wall when he couldn't operate the new can opener.

Change: even some of the things that had changed for Gma. Not just the music—now it really rocked, Aretha Franklin's "Think," Big Brother and the Holding Company's "Piece of My Heart," Marvin Gaye's "What's Going On," Canned Heat, Toots and the Maytals, Joe Cocker, the Who, hard music with voices almost shouting—but even what she was doing with her days. He didn't understand the unrest at home. The antiwar protests, the civil rights marches, the mayhem in the streets of Chicago at the Democratic convention. Even in Ithaca, the students from the Afro-American Society had taken over Willard Straight Hall at Cornell. She'd been there on the lawn outside supporting them and the SDS protesters on the front steps.

"I'm fighting the war at home for you," she told him. "If you were fighting for freedom over there, I was going to do it back here. Otherwise, what were you fighting for, Charlie? I was doing it for you. I was doing it for us. I was doing it for everyone I considered an American. What are we fighting for if we say we're fighting for freedom and democracy in Vietnam, but we don't fight for it here at home?"

Days passed. Weeks. The National Guard hosed protesters in California with skin-stinging spray from helicopters. Riots erupted in downtown Manhattan outside the Stonewall Inn after an assault on gay Americans. The summer spun and he tried to listen to Gma. In July, human beings walked on the moon. Nothing seemed the same. Nothing was the same.

"Charlie," Gma kept telling him. "The way for us to find each other again is for you to trust that I've been keeping your home worth something while you were out risking your life for ours. I love you. Let me show you how I loved you."

And he did. He believed her. What else could he do? He didn't recognize his own home—all he recognized was the woman he had promised he would come home to.

This is how Gpa finishes telling the story this time: "This is what I'm always saying, Teddy. The point of living is learning how to love." He pauses, then continues. "Your grandmother. She lived with love, boy. She was love. That's what I called her until the day she died, that was her name to me: Love. I'll call her that until the day I die." Then he pauses and looks at me. "Won't I?"

It's nearly seven as we cross a few short bridges over the Meramec River and Butler Lakes in the southernmost reaches of the St. Louis metropolitan area. We need gas and food and because it has taken all day to get here, we have no plan for the night.

"We need to get to Ithaca tomorrow," I say.

"I don't think we can," Corrina says.

"Let's just drive through the night."

"I can't do that."

"We'll take turns."

"I don't think you should drive anymore," Corrina says. I'm about to take offense at this when I realize she's looking out for me; however silly and small the notion, it's still her saying *I care for you.*

We can't cut through St. Louis, but we do think we can get back on a real highway, the 70, northwest of St. Louis, in Illinois, and on the 70, we can get across Illinois, Indiana, Ohio, and into Pennsylvania without paying a toll. Beyond that New York State waits for us with whatever else is there, and if we make it there, at least we can sit on the steps of the church and say, "Here, Gpa, right here. This is where you and Gma got married. Tell us the story. Tell us so we know you remember."

But right where we have to pick up the 70 to make that last long leg of the journey is the little city I've been trying to imagine since I first heard about it in Las Vegas, and the woman, CC, who's too close for me not to go find her. I feel like Dead Dad, renavigating my course, wanting nothing more than to chase the rhumb line to CC.

We've merged onto a larger road and have joined traffic heading to a bridge. It's the Mississippi. Once we cross it, we're in the flat, green wash of Illinois. The sun is low behind us. The west is a blur of red, yellow, and orange through the rear window, and yet somehow, my past is ahead of me, waiting just up the road, the ghost of Dead Dad.

All too many days at school, in my lonesome daze, his ghost would haunt my daydreams. I'd be thinking about one thing in geometry or bio or English class, and then my mind would drift, and I'd be half asleep and the nightmare would surface of a tsunami hitting the California coast, the school submerged in the flood, and Dead Dad's giant pale arms surging, rising up and crashing down on us like the crests of enormous waves, pulling the whole school down with him to his watery grave.

I'm a windblown mess inside and I look back at Gpa, hoping he'll brace me, hoping, I realize, he'll keep up the family lie, so I don't have to face what I'm heading straight for.

"Let's skip it," I say suddenly. "Let's just push on. I don't want to do this."

"What?" Corrina says.

"We need to get to New York. I can't stop us." I'm trembling.

"Do you know what pisses me off?" Corrina says, almost shouting at me. "Here you are. You have a chance to find something out about your dad."

"I don't have a dad," I say, and I hate how I sound like a baby.

"Yes you do. He was someone. He still is someone. You could find out more."

"What am I going to do? Go look at his grave? He's buried in Ithaca, anyway."

"You have to go talk to her."

No, I think, but that's not what I say. "Yes. I know."

"Good," she says bitterly. "Because you know I would, if I could. You're right here, Hendrix." Her voice cracks, and I think about how much of an asshole I am.

"Okay." I nod at Corrina. "I'm ready. We just have to figure out how to find her."

I know this is going to be strange for Gpa, too. How could it not be? And I'm turning around to talk to him, to begin to explain why I need to do this, why it has been on my mind for so long and now, with the Blue Bomber gliding so close to the source, I have to learn a story I fear no one but CC can help me know, when Gpa leans forward and puts his hand on my shoulder.

"I know she's in Troy because she sent me flowers when your grandmother died. She'd already moved here. Found a job in St. Louis shortly after your father died. She said she was sorry. I never wrote her back. I should have."

I'm speechless. It's all I can do to get air in and out of my nose.

Old Humper is in tune with the moment, because he, too, is sitting up and alert, watching me and Gpa. He whimpers slightly and then nuzzles Gpa's side. Gpa takes his hand off my shoulder and gives Old Humper some attention, and I stare out the window.

Eventually I find some words in my throat. "Do you blame her?" I ask. "For his death?"

"No."

"Did you then?"

"I'm not sure. I was angry, but I don't think I blamed her. I don't think it was her fault."

"Why not?"

"Your father was the one who was out here. He was the one who traveled back and forth to be with her. I blame him for being out here or there, or wherever. But I don't blame her or him or anyone else for his death. I've seen too many die to go looking for reasons why every time. Why cancer? Why war? Why a car accident? Why do we die? That isn't a question for an old man. I'd rather ask myself what I'm doing while I'm still here."

I sit with this for a long time. We get gas, we find our way onto the 70, the last straight line east to where we set out to go, but we coast on it for the short stretch from Collinsville to exit 18, Route 162. Corrina pulls the Blue Bomber into the right lane, takes the off-ramp, finds Edwardsville Road, and within minutes her phone tells us we're there.

Troy is everything LA is not. If there is a town here, we can't locate it. Scattered low buildings, a few streetlights. There is nothing to see but the magnificent bowl of infinite night enclosing the world around us. In the mostly darkness, without a city's light pollution, without any other cars on the road, with only the land and the sky and us in between, I realize that this is what most of the country is like, a sea of land that wants you to get lost in it. I am a city kid, and I think the city hides the majesty of the universe too easily. But not out here. Out here, I am reminded of the ancient Greek word *poiesis*, the root of the word *poetry*. It basically means *making something out of nothing*. And out here, in what I once would have called the middle of nowhere, I am reminded of humility, because out here I am reminded of how small and insignificant I am, and yet, in the face of that, I want to make poetry. I want to make a life that could mean nothing, mean *something* instead.

CHAPTER 24

CC's Story

It isn't easy to find someone's address, but it is when their name is their business and it looks like they work from home—at least according to the website. It'd be strange if there was more than one Cecelia Devons, and the one we want to find wasn't the owner of CC's Farm, right out there at the edge of town.

Her house is down a winding street that takes us back out into farmland. A short, chipped wooden fence runs along one side of the road, a ditch with hedges along the other. There are no streetlights and a few lonely trees loom over the road. There is a slight breeze, and the trees' limbs dance and seem to laugh in the glare of our headlights. Soon there are no other houses, only the road, and the map says the road is about to end. No cul-de-sac, no housing development, just the end of the road.

We slow as we approach the end of the pavement. Nothing extends from it, not a dirt road, not a bridge, nothing, just grass and a field and whatever lies beyond the reach of the headlights. And then we see it. Off to the left, hidden behind the final hedge, sits the dark wooden house, with two front windows glowing. There's a driveway up to the garage, but we don't use it. Corrina parks out front, pointing the car back where we came from.

"Are you ready?" she asks.

"No."

We all get out, but we leave Old Humper in the car for now, with the windows down enough so he can breathe. We're not sure what to expect and we might have to get out of here quickly. Gpa's walking slowly, shuffling, as we climb the slight rise to the house. An invisible cloud of barnyard smell hovers everywhere around us. The low bleating of sheep or goats, the grunt of a pig—we can't see them, but they are out there, and it is almost magical in the darkness. The buzz and hum of the insects and the wind rustling the hedges and the cornstalks in the field to our right bring us back into the moment.

I kiss Corrina on the cheek just before we get to the front steps. "I'm glad you're here," I tell her. "I couldn't be here right now without you."

"I'm glad I'm here too," she says.

Gpa walks up the steps, and I follow, but when we get to the door he hesitates. I ring the bell when I realize he isn't going to do it.

At first there's nothing. We hear only the noises from

outside the house, but then there's something like the sound of voices, and the curtain in the window beside the door parts and a girl a few years younger than me looks out onto the porch. She steps back when the front door opens, and she leans into the embrace of the woman who stares at us.

When she looks at me she smiles and there is so much sadness in her eyes I can't help but feel wrecked myself. "Charlie?" she asks. "Ted?" She nods to us. "I guess we've been expecting you."

They must be mother and daughter, standing there in their matching jeans and flannel shirts, cuffs rolled to the elbows like they were just at work, hair pulled into ponytails the color of the rails of the wooden fence along the road. They are a unit and they move as one, same tilt in their heads as they look at us, same knowing pity in the hooks of their sad smiles. Yet there's something more about the girl that bothers me, but in that moment of silence I only hear Gpa's words in my head.

"Ted Hendrix," I say. I introduce Corrina and Gpa. "Can we come in?"

CC leads us to the living room, introduces us to her daughter, Rose, and stares at Corrina. "They didn't say anything about her. Although they wondered if there'd be a driver."

"They?" Corrina asks.

"Who?" But I already know the answer before I ask.

"The police. They called here earlier this evening. They had a hunch you were heading out this way."

"Ithaca," I say.

CC nods. She and Rose sit together in an armchair. CC sits leaning forward, and Rose perches on the cushioned arm. They remain huddled close, watching us.

"I'm sorry the cops called."

"What are you doing here?"

"I'm not sure," I say. "I think I need to know a few things." I can see the fear in her and in Rose, too. "We're not crazy," I add.

But then I tell her a crazy story. I tell her about how on a hillside just five days ago, Corrina and I decided to make this trip together, and about how Gpa's Alzheimer's eats away at his brain and his memories and how I want to get him back to Ithaca one last time to see the church in which he got married before the disease takes it and his memory of Gma away from him forever, and how it isn't fair that in a world that takes our loved ones away so easily, this can happen too, that not only do you lose the ones you love, but you can lose all memory of them too, as if they never existed at all. And I pull the HFB from the pocket of my cargo shorts and I hold it in the air above my head like some biblical scroll and I tell her how I have to get it all down, because when disease and death come to take it all away, at least we'll have a record of how we lived and who lived with us while we were here.

I tell her the book has a hole in it and I need to fill it and she's the only person left in the world who can do that, but as I'm talking like a madman I'm looking at Rose and wondering what about her looks so damn familiar, until it finally dawns on me.

"How old are you?" I ask.

"Ten," she says, looking back at me with those same ocean-blue eyes of mine and Gpa's and also Dead Dad's, and I think about how the world that seemed so impossibly large an hour ago seems so much smaller in an instant.

"She's your half sister," CC says. "But I never thought the two of you would meet."

I look from Rose to CC. "No secrets here," CC says.

"You live in LA," Rose says. "Where my dad was from." And in her shy voice, I again feel all that distance between here and there.

"Yes," I say. "I'm sorry." I point at Gpa. "This is your grandfather." She doesn't leave the chair; she presses closer to her mother, instead. I put my hand on Gpa's knee. "Did you know?" I ask.

He squints at me and pushes my hand off his knee. "I don't understand," he says. "What's going on?"

"Gpa," I say.

"Don't Gpa me," he says, raising his voice.

"No, Gpa, please. Please." I glance at Rose and CC. "It's okay," I tell them.

"I just don't understand," Gpa says again. "What am I doing here?"

Corrina gets up and kneels beside him. She rubs his back gently, and although he looks at her like he's never seen her

255

before, he accepts her comfort. She starts to hum softly. "Maybe we should go out to the car?" she asks me.

"But . . ." I say without being able to finish, because I don't know what I want to say.

"It's okay," she says. "I'd like to take him outside. This is all making me a little sad anyway."

I want to help her, not because I want to make sure Gpa calms down—I trust her with that more than myself now—but because I want to help her. I want us to arrive at answers together, but we can't because we're two separate people with two very different lives, and the best I can do is to promise to do for her what she has done for me.

Corrina walks Gpa outside and I know she's helping him back down the stairs and down the slope to the Blue Bomber, where she'll talk with him a bit and then pull out her guitar and play the same songs she sings to the ex-hippies back in LA, songs that were sung in a time when people still thought they could change the world.

In the living room I explain how this happens with Gpa, especially at night, and when he's confronted with too many conflicting emotions or decisions. I sound like Dr. Hannaway, but younger and so much dumber.

"You need to get him back in the right care," CC says. "You can't do this all on your own, Ted."

I like that she calls me Ted. I do feel like a new man, in some way. "I will," I say. "I will." I lean forward on the couch. "But isn't there anything else you can tell me about my father?

I mean, our father?" I say, looking at Rose. "When he died, was he coming to say good-bye to you or was he coming to stay with you?"

"I don't know," CC says. She lets go of Rose and stands. She moves to the fireplace and leans on the mantel, looking into the empty hearth. "I don't think he wanted to choose."

She and my mom are as different as Troy and LA. Where Mom is all angles and frantic gestures, CC is soft and slow. She isn't wearing makeup. There's muscle in her arms and legs, not just bone. And yet, even with all these miles between them, I think about how much they are alike.

I think about CC raising Rose on her own and I think about Mom raising me. All those years she could have gone on dates, but instead sat on the couch with me, reading aloud, or later, asking me to read aloud to her—date night with her ten-year-old son standing on the ottoman, shouting lines from an old, worn copy of *The Hobbit*. Mom worked her ass off, and mostly for my sake, and she might have been a pain in the ass back home, but in the real world, out where the armies of moms and dads marched on through the boredom and sadness of discarded dreams, she was one of the heroes. I think: *I came all this way to find him, but maybe I just found her—my mom, Penny Weaver, someone else whose story should be remembered, the mother who's been struggling to keep it all together and has.*

"The last time he came to see me," CC says, "I told him I was pregnant. I told him I wanted to keep her. He was happy. He was terrified. We sat on the back steps of the old café where I used to work and he kissed me. He was always too afraid to kiss me in public." Tears slip down her cheek. "I'm sorry," she says. She's speaking to Rose, not me, and Rose gets out of the chair she's now slumped in and goes over to her mother. She puts her arms around her mother and sighs, I can see it in her shoulders, and I wonder how many times she's been the one to comfort her mother, how many times she's said, in something as simple as a hug, *This is why we go on, this is why we wake to another day.*

"But after your grandfather saw us," CC continues, "your dad said we'd talk about it more. He said he had to go back to LA because your grandfather would do exactly what he said he would do, and call your mother." She sniffles. "So I don't know, Ted. I don't know. I don't know if he was going back to LA to stay with your mother, or if he was going back to LA to break it off with your mother. He died, and he left you and your mother, and he left me and my little jelly bean. That's what I called her when I told your father about her, the little jelly bean, because at that point she was no bigger than one."

"Or if he was going to try to make it all work out for everyone, even though he couldn't," I say.

"Yes, Ted. That was your father. He was stupid, but he wasn't heartless." Then she turned to me. "Ted? The police called me. They know you're somewhere out around here. I don't know anything about Corrina, but think about your grandfather. Think about your mother."

"I know," I say. *I contain multitudes,* Walt Whitman says, and in so many ways Gpa, Dead Dad, and I are three versions of the same man. We are one dead, one dying, and one alive with the choice of what to make of the rest of his life. We are dead so much longer than we are alive, dead for nearly all of eternity, really, and life, then, is a flash of light, a rebellion against the tyranny of dark nothingness, like one of Corrina's solar flares leaping off the surface, burning bright but briefly, before falling again into the fire—life itself is a poem, and what we make of it is our poetry.

CHAPTER 25

"We Fight for What We Love, Not Are"

It's much later and CC has offered the living room as a place for us to crash for the night. Corrina and Gpa are back, and he's stretched out on the couch, barely awake. He was mostly frightened, not angry, when we brought him back in, and I think I understand. I'm too tired for anger too. Anger takes so much out of us. As I sit on the floor, with my back against the couch and Old Humper's head in my lap, and I listen to Corrina sing and play another tune for us all, I feel warm and calm. I'm grateful to be here now.

"You have the loveliest voice," CC tells Corrina when she's finished. "Is that your own song?"

"Yes."

"It's beautiful," CC says.

Corrina shakes her head. There's something like sadness in her smile. "Nah."

"Hey," CC says. "I'm serious. You need to keep this up."

"Yeah," Corrina says softly, but she stares down into her

lap. "Thing is—" She stops. I don't think I've ever seen Corrina really cry before, and now, here, of all places, she's on the verge of it.

"Would you mind if Corrina and I take Skipper out for a short walk?" I ask CC. "Want to let him stretch his legs and whatnot before we're down for the night. We won't be gone long."

"Can I come?" Rose asks.

"No," CC tells Rose. She gives me a knowing mom smile—one I can appreciate right now. "We're going to stay here and make sure your grandfather doesn't wake up alone." And when she says that, I realize she's talking to me and Rose. He's our grandfather. Rose has never known any of her Dead Dad's family.

"When we get back," I say to Rose, "I'll tell you all about him."

"Who?"

"Your grandfather."

But first: Corrina. Old Humper's on a leash, but as soon as we're down the steps and the slope and standing behind the Blue Bomber and looking into the darkened meadow beyond the end of the road, I drop the leash and let him run. Old Humper needs to get his freak on. I can see it in the way his legs shake as he stretches on the grass. He doesn't get far. He heads back up the road to a stump by the hedges. While he's going at it, I put my arm around Corrina. She's remained quiet since we walked out the door. She's still not speaking.

"Hey," I say.

She turns her head into the crook of my shoulder. "I'll never have this," she says. "Not even in New York."

I'm trying to find words, but what can I say that won't sound cheap and painful? I hold her.

She turns away, looks into the field, but remains in my arm, up against me. "It doesn't matter anyway. We're not going to make it to New York."

"No," I say. "We're not."

"I hate LA. I just want one shot somewhere else. I just wanted to get to New York with a clean slate, where nobody knew me. I just wanted one shot to wow someone."

"You still can."

"What, with Aiko? She texted back. *Look me up,* she said. It could be real. It might just be casual chitchat. Doesn't matter. We're never going to make it there."

I rub her shoulder and hold her tight. I lean us back against the Blue Bomber's trunk. "If you knock on her door, she's not going to turn you away."

"Yeah, well, it's over anyway" She nestles her head against me, still gazing out in front of us. "I just didn't want this all to end."

"It doesn't have to," I say. It is an absolutely clear night and the Big Dipper, the Little Dipper, Cassiopeia, and Pegasus all glitter and glow in a perfectly painted still life on the underside of the umbrella of the sky that hovers above us, but I think there is a way to tear through that fabric and find something greater. And yet, as if the sky has dropped right down into the field, or we have floated right up into those stars, as I look out across the field I see fireflies flickering in the darkness. They're innumerable, but if I draw a line between one here and there, I can make my own constellation of the two of us—Corrina & Hendrix—just one new design woven into the oldest cloth there is.

I can feel Corrina's heart hammering in her chest against my body, and there is nothing more I want to do than keep alive the music of her desire, and it is something more than me. Because if you love someone, and you've heard her say *Hey, this is who I want to be,* again and again, your job is to stand up and give a hand to get her there.

I've spent so much time trying to get down all the stories, thinking that the stories that feel the truest are the ones during which we learn who we are—and sometimes those are the stories about where we're from, but sometimes they're the ones we write ourselves. The ones about where we're going.

"You don't have to stop here," I say. "You should go on without us."

Corrina pulls away and looks up at me.

"Get a ticket to New York. The rest of the money we have—we'll pool it. It should be enough to get you there and let you kick around a bit."

"I can't do that."

"You can. Someone has to make it."

"But we started this together. I can't go alone."

"You won't be alone. Not forever. You just have to get there and see what happens. It's not about the money," I add. "I promised you I'd help you get somewhere, and one thing I can do is keep a promise. Especially one I made to you. Go to Brooklyn. See what happens. I believe in you."

Because here is something else I now know about love. You have to see the person who is there, not the person who is not. You have to believe in the person who is there, not the person who is not. You have to love the person who is there, and not the person who is not.

She looks out to the field and I can see the excitement in her eyes. "Yes?"

"Yes."

"Yes."

"Yes."

And then, leaning against the curve of the Blue Bomber, we are kissing. Why do we say we're falling for someone when the feeling sings and swirls so much more like flying? We kiss and kiss, and not like before, it is something more, like the kisses themselves are new words in a new language, and the way she holds my lip with hers, the way I hold hers with mine, I'm sure I've sailed right home into the uncertain I was always looking to find.

We have to call Old Humper from his business and head back into CC's house, and when we do, we find her and Rose in the living room again. They've thrown a blanket over Gpa and arranged some blankets and pillows and sleeping bags on the floor.

"Rose wants to know if she can camp in here with you tonight," CC says to me when we've taken off our shoes and tucked ourselves back against the couch again.

"Of course," Corrina and I both say.

"And I owe you a story," I tell Rose.

Rose smiles and wraps one of the blankets around her shoulders. She snuggles herself into a ball in the armchair and rests her head on the wide arm she sat on earlier as I pull the HFB from the pocket of my cargo shorts and open it to the very beginning, ready to read just the parts about Gpa and Gma, so Rose can hear what I've tried to piece together: *The Last True Love Story in the Hendrix Family Book.*

"I always wanted a little sister," Corrina says. "I wanted someone to protect, or at least to give some advice to. About everything I had to face."

"Well," I say, "please help me, because I guess I have a sister."

"I will," Corrina says. "I will."

CC stands in the doorway, leaning against the dark wooden frame. Behind me, Gpa's asleep beneath a thick plaid blanket. Rose's eyes are wide and waiting. Corrina's squeezed herself under my arm, so I have to hug her while I hold the book open with my other hand. Old Humper's curled up on the other side of me with his head on my knee. A red lamp burns in the corner of the room and it's all the light I need. But before I begin reading the HFB aloud, I scribble an epigraph on the front cover. It's a line from a Frank O'Hara poem that's been floating in the mist just beyond my memory for the entire trip and finally emerges now: *"We fight for what we love, not are."*

CHAPTER 26

ITHACA

In the morning, CC shakes me awake, and even though my eyes are open, I'm taking in the room around me. I don't remember falling asleep, but someone kindly put the HFB on the coffee table nearby with my pen resting right on top. CC puts her finger to her lips and beckons me to follow her to the kitchen. The local news plays on low volume.

"You were just on it," she says. "There's a Silver Alert out for Charlie. The police are looking for you and him. Please. You have to go right now. I don't want any trouble. The cops called last night and I don't want any trouble for me and Rose. Please."

"Okay," I say. I'm barely awake. "Can I say good-bye to Rose?"

She thinks about this.

"What I mean is a good-bye for now."

She hugs me tightly and I immediately think of Mom and what she must be thinking right this second—now that she's back in LA. I have so many stories to tell her, but I should be home to tell them to her.

"Is there a bus stop in town?" I ask CC. "Any way to keep going? To get to New York?"

"No, you have to stop, Ted."

"We will. Gpa and I will turn ourselves in. But I want to keep my promise to Corrina. She doesn't have to stop just because we do."

"You take the number thirteen bus. That'll get you to Glen Carbon, and from there you can get to Alton, where you can pick up an Amtrak to anywhere in the country. But just so you know, I'm going to call the police as soon as you leave. I'll say I don't know where you're going, because I don't, and I don't want to know."

Ithaca, I think, but not really. It's as if Ithaca doesn't even exist anymore, gone, lost in the fog of memories, like a memory itself, a thing you can't hold or touch, or even really see—and only your faith in the story of it keeps it alive.

We wake everyone up, and even though it's morning, when Gpa is usually at his best, he's still a little confused, and Corrina takes him and Old Humper outside. I hug CC and Rose. We agree this is the beginning of something weird but honest, something that will continue, but not right now, and I promise I'll see them both again. With the morning light reaching into the ocean of the sky, Corrina lets loose the Blue Bomber, and we glide back out onto the road one last time.

We're all quiet as we drive into town. Corrina's face is the moon, soft and distant in the blue morning sky. She has Jimi Hendrix playing now and she doesn't have to tell me it's her favorite of his, the soft acoustic version of "Hear My Train A Comin'." Those high warbling notes that swoop around each other like one swallow chasing another, but then drop and roll, birds no more, more footsteps slow and heavy, dragging a dusty blues at their heels. Corrina's singing along softly, harmonizing with Jimi, but I still hear her now just like the first time I heard her voice sail out into the LA sky.

The bus stop isn't a station. It's a white rectangle painted on the side of the road in front of an appliance store and across the street from the small, windowless Municipal Building. There are advertisements for Whirlpool everywhere, and I feel like I'm stuck in one, spinning and spinning, and soon I'll be pulled down into the vortex, sucked back to LA. At least Corrina will make it, even if she has to go alone.

We park the Blue Bomber in the empty lot across the street and wait for the 8 a.m. bus. It'll be here any minute, and I explain what I learned from CC, and how Corrina's going to get all the way to Penn Station in New York. She listens and nods. We sit awkwardly in the front seats until Corrina realizes she should grab her bag and guitar, in case the bus only pulls over for a moment. We get out of the car.

Two other people have come out from the street behind the appliance store and stand by the pole with the bus sign on it. Another car pulls into the lot. A few people head into the Municipal Building. And then we both see the bus coming down the road.

"I need to do this," Corrina says. "I need to try. For me."

"You need to go," I agree.

"I'll find you when I'm back."

"I believe you."

"No. I will."

"I believe you."

"I'm not just saying that, Hendrix."

"Corrina," I say. The wind lifts her hair around her face. I tuck some of it behind her ear. "I believe you." We kiss.

"And I need a favor," she says. "Please tell the ex-hippies I'll be back. I'll be back in time for school. For Rosewood. I will."

"I will. And I'll get my license."

"You better."

"To come see you at school. I'll come every weekend."

"You better."

"To spring you from that prison."

"Yes."

"We're good at that."

"Yes."

We kiss again, until we hear Gpa behind us.

"She's going to miss the bus," he says, standing on the

other side of the car, arms folded and resting on the roof. He smiles. "Get out of here."

"I'll see you back at home," I say to Corrina.

She hoists her bag on her back, picks up her guitar, and walks to the curb. She turns, standing there, sunglasses catching the light, same twilight bandana tying back her hair as it did that first day on the road. "You and me, Hendrix?" she says. "Badass."

"Yes."

"Yes."

And then she's across the street and disappears behind the bus. The windows are tinted so I can't see where she sits, but I imagine her putting her boot up on the seat in front of her, guitar in her lap, frets by her ear, tuning, ready to sing to the world.

Gpa and I stand across the car from each other, and then he comes around so we can both watch the bus pull away from the curb. He has Old Humper by the leash.

"I'm sorry," I tell him. "I'm sorry I couldn't get us to Ithaca."

He puts his arm around me. "Teddy," he says. "Did I ever tell you about how your grandmother and I got married?"

"Ahh! I know. That's where I was trying to get us, Gpa. I'm sorry. I really am."

"That was just for our parents. We got married before that. Just the two of us. The hill where we first went. On our nondate? Betty asked if we could get married there first.

Just us, none of all the nonsense. Of course, I said. My little romantic. She was so convincing. The rest of our life will be our public promise, she said. Let's let one moment, one night, be ours, and ours alone. It was just us and the stars above. She was right, she was always right, at least for me, and so we snuck out the night before our wedding at St. Helen's. She wore a cotton dress with the simplest little frills along the hemline, and I wore her favorite brown corduroys of mine, and a tie, I had to wear a tie, for me. She brought a blanket this time, and we spread it out just as we did that first night. Anyway, we said our words, and the moonlight through the leaves of the trees was just like stained glass in the church anyway, but black and white and gray, and that was the real thing for me. And boy oh boy did we kiss. No holding back that night. We kissed with the whole world around us, alive. I can see the moonlight on her face even now."

He holds me as he tells me and he knows damn well I'm thinking about Corrina just like he's thinking about Gma.

"Teddy," he says, poking me in the chest. "Ithaca is here. With us."

EPILOGUE

Here's the situation: We're stuck on a bench in the Municipal Building in Troy, Illinois, and even though I've never been so far away from home, I've never felt so close to it. The bench reminds me of the bench in the hall outside the administrative offices back at school, back where I'll be in a month. It's a worn yellowed wood the color of the world's most watered-down honey, and it's up against the same boring concrete wall, and whether I'm here or there, both are lifeless without Corrina and her voice, and her smile, and her glance, and her pulse.

They got us. After Corrina drifted away on her bus, *they* came out of the building shouting and waving their laminated badges. The police car parked beside us and *they* walked us inside, sat us on the bench, and stood over us in their water cooler shirtsleeves and their corkboard ties. *They* spoke into telephones, and pulled at their beards, and Gpa and I sat on the bench, smiling like idiots with our hands between our knees. *They* came and *they* got us, just like we maybe always knew *they* would.

But I'm not worried now, and neither is Gpa. He must look like the Alzheimer's patient everyone knows he is, but they must think I'm the crazy one here. And I am, and I'm okay with that. *They* got us, but Gpa's humming to himself, almost rocking himself to a rhythm, and I know he's not really here on the bench, he's in his Ithaca, because I finally finished the poem and just gave it to him, and he's reading and rereading it.

The new plan: We have to try to get him to memorize it, just like all those songs lyrics he remembers—so that he remembers what he already knows and has taught me, that *every love story is an odyssey.*

WHAT MATTERS

It's not about how long ago,
  It feels like yesterday.
The first time you saw her eyes
  Look at you that way.
You knew in your gut so certainly,
  But were too afraid to flatter,
Because anyone can fall in love,
  It's the staying in that matters.

Suddenly you got your chance again
  When you were at her house,
You in your fraying tie,
  Betty her faded blouse,
And she took you to the hillside by the lake,
  Away from Ithaca's chatter,
Because anyone can fall in love,
  It's the staying in that matters.

So you went, again and again,
    It was your favorite place,
Staring at your reflections between the stars
    In the long, glass-still lake,
"Go ahead and throw your rock," she said,
    "The two of us won't shatter,"
Because anyone can fall in love,
    It's the staying in that matters.

And under the moon-white tree,
    Betty stood with moon-wet hair,
She held her steady gaze and promised,
    "Like the moon, I'll always be there,"
That's when you fumbled with the ring,
    And fumbled how you asked her,
Because anyone can fall in love,
    It's the staying in that matters.

And so when the rest of your life
    Feels like one long war,
Where the giants, ghosts, and witches you meet
    Are always chasing after more,
Remember you and Betty have built a home
    That holds against any storm that gathers,
Because anyone can fall in love,
    It's the staying in that matters.

But I slip off to my Ithaca too, because when I open the HFB to record the last story Gpa told me outside, the one about the two of them up against the world to come, I flip to the back and find an entry I didn't write. It's in Corrina's handwriting:

THE STORY OF HOW
CORRINA AND HENDRIX FELL IN LOVE

ACKNOWLEDGMENTS

This story is extremely personal to me, and I want to thank everyone in the Kiely family who supported me and put me on a plane to Ireland to travel the south and west coasts with my uncle Bob and my Grandma and Grandpa Kiely, a trip that made me realize how much a young person can learn about love from the generations ahead of him—even when, and maybe especially when, Grandpa had Alzheimer's, had his bad moments, told stories that wandered off track, often got lost, but still closed with a punch line about why he loved who he loved.

Thank you to Linsey Abrams and Felicia Bonaparte, the powerful godmothers of my graduate school, who guided me out of the doldrums of my life with their love of literature. This book began in their co-taught Narrative Structures class, in which we were supposed to write the first chapter of a book we'd never finish, and for which I didn't follow the rules, because I wrote the book and that first chapter is now long gone. We learn the rules to break them, don't we?

The book would have remained a dream, however, without the help of three men foolhardy enough to stick by me in adventure after adventure. Thank you Steve Rosenstein for scraping me off the floor in Las Vegas and driving us all the way to St. Louis, getting lost, and finding Lotus Eaters and a

Cyclops along the way. That trip made the book and I'll owe you forever. And thank you Ted Boretti for the first road trip and the second, and the countless quixotic trips between and after, and for always philosophizing with me deep into the night and teaching me that enthusiasm is a muscle that needs to be exercised. And thank you Perry Hendrix, for, no matter the distance between us, always putting the friendship first and for reminding me why we love what we do and that we must buckle down and do it.

Thank you Matt Kudish for your invaluable discussions about Alzheimer's. So much of what you taught me is in the book, and even more importantly, contains life lessons about love that I hope this book does some justice to. Thank you Brenna Larson for your wisdom and compassion for this story. And thanks to Nina Czitrom, Allie Jane Bruce, Jason Reynolds, and Daniel José Older, whose early reads helped me think and write more thoughtfully—I'm deeply grateful for your friendships and generosity.

This book would also have been a wandering mess without the help of David Groff. Thank you, as always, for your deft guidance and inspiring encouragement. And thank you Rob Weisbach, who, more than an agent, as a friend always reminds me to get out of the head and back into the heart—it's the home I'm aiming for, and I'm so grateful for your steering me back there. And thank you to the whole S&S and Margaret K. McElderry team—especially Ruta Rimas, whose wisdom and excitement I am so grateful to partner with on